ROGUE

CALLIE HART

ROGUE

Formatting by Max Henry of Max Effect
    www.formaxeffect.com

LIVE FOR SOMETHING
OR DIE FOR NOTHING

For *ALICE*, for being the best bitch in town.

For *RYAN*, for shutting down every bar in Sydney with me.

For *ANDY*, for every single cringe-worthy pun.

For *ASTRID* & *CAMPBELL*. There isn't enough wine and cheese in the world.

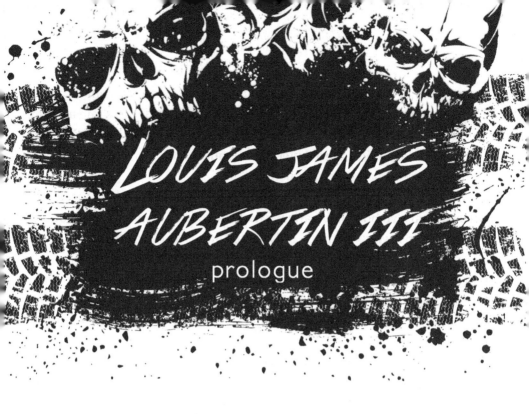

LOUIS JAMES AUBERTIN III

prologue

"**Y**ou're a fucking embarrassment, you know that don't you? I can't believe you're my goddamn son. If you hadn't been born within the walls of this house, I'd think the wrong child had been brought home from the hospital."

My father throws back the last of his champagne and hands off the empty glass to one of his faceless servants. Faceless to him, but not to me. I know Sarah, know that she just became a grandmother for the first time this morning and no matter how badly my father treats her today, even he won't be able to keep the smile off her face. She gives me a wry shrug, placing the glass carefully on her silver tray, and then she vanishes off into the crowd.

My father is oblivious to the entire exchange. "You had no business inviting people here this evening, James. This is a political event. There are important people here. Serious people. Your little friends aren't suitable company for you to be keeping. You're not a child anymore. Lord knows you might still act like it, but you're not."

I dig my fingernails into my palms, though the action is hidden inside the pockets of the four thousand dollar Ralph Lauren suit I'm wearing. The suit he made me wear. "Cade Preston is a veteran, the same as I am, Dad. He served his country for four years in one of the most dangerous places on earth. And Laura's just been made partner at her father's law firm. How are they not *serious* people?"

My father scoffs. "Cade followed you to the other side of the world because you two boys have always had ridiculous, romanticized notions of war. That's why you both only lasted for two tours. Neither of you accepted the rank owed to you because of your station. You went out there, full of piss and vinegar, thinking it would be easier to start at the bottom rung, where you'd have no responsibility. And then you didn't like it, didn't want to stick it out, so you quit and came home before the job was done."

Louis James Aubertin II loves baiting me like this in public. He knows if he says these things to me in a crowd, there's nothing I can do but grin and take it from him. Makes him feel big. Superior. Thing is, my tolerance for this kind of treatment is wearing really fucking thin. "The U.S Marine Corp is not *the bottom rung*. The Marines are an elite unit. It takes an insane amount of hard work and dedication to even get in. If you think I had no responsibility as a Marine, then you clearly have very little understanding of how the United States Military is run." I don't bother defending the length of time my friend and I spent barely surviving out in the desert. What would be the point? Old Louis has no fucking clue. He'd simply say I was making excuses for myself. He can't possibly comprehend what four long, never-ending years in that environment is like. How the dirt and the sand and the hostile locals and the poverty and the disease and the heat and the IEDs and the amputations and the Taliban and the rape victims and the pain and the suffering all eventually wear you down.

My father's eyes flash with the same unbridled fury I've been provoking in him for years. "I was there in Vietnam, you little shit," he spits. "I was there from the moment the war started until the moment it ended. Don't you tell me I have no idea how the U.S. military works."

Yes, Old Louis was in Vietnam, and yes he was there from start to finish, but he has nothing to be proud of. He never held a rifle or got his hands dirty a single day of that war. He sat with his other command buddies in a hotel fifty miles away from the jungle, where the only conflict they ever encountered was when the toilet paper was too rough to wipe their pampered, lily white asses on.

I say all of this in my head, but the thoughts don't make it out of my mouth. I press my tongue firmly against the back of my front teeth, just in case a rogue insult should try and escape me. This is how it's been for years now. So many fucking years. Our mutual hatred of one another only magnifies itself as time passes. I hate him because he's a vile, angry, malicious old man. He hates me because I killed my mother.

Fair turnaround.

In truth, I hate myself for killing my mother too, but there wasn't much to be done about it at the time. I had to be born, and fate decided to take the woman who carried me in her womb for nine months, only three seconds after I came kicking and screaming into the world. It was entirely unintentional on my part.

My father swoops down on another of the wait staff, Gavin this time, and snatches up a fresh glass of champagne without uttering a word of thanks. "And what about the girl? Laura Preston is a brash young woman who doesn't know when to hold her tongue. She's only made partner at her father's firm because it's exactly that—*her father's firm.* She wouldn't have accomplished anything if she'd had to fend for herself, James. There's no denying that. And just...just look at what she's wearing, for crying out loud. She looks like a fucking prostitute." He points off across the other side of the room to where Laura, Cade's sister, is laughing with a young guy I don't know, her head tipped back as she lets out a throaty bark of amusement. Her blonde, cropped hair has been pinned up out of her face—a minor miracle, considering it's normal, wild state—and there's the faintest hint of blush reddening her cheeks. She always said she'd never wear make up when we were growing up, and for a long time she didn't. She doesn't need it, and she's sure as hell never been a girly girl, but tonight she looks great with that tiny splash of color brightening her face.

3

The dress she's wearing is decked out in gold sequins, which reflect the light from the illuminated chandeliers overheard, sending fragments of golden, fiery light dancing and skittering on the walls and on the ceiling. It's not something a respectable Alabama woman would wear in polite company, and that is precisely why she's worn it. I want to high-five her so badly, but that sort of behavior would be frowned upon.

"As soon as the speeches are over, I want the three of you out of here. You understand me? I don't care where you go. Just make sure you're not on the property. God knows what'll happen if the three of you start drinking."

I bare my teeth at my father, arranging my face into a rictus of false civility. "Gladly." Little does my father know, I've already started drinking and I have zero intention of fucking stopping. That would be a really dumb idea at this point in the proceedings. After all, the speeches won't be for another hour. I have to survive this ridiculous circus until then, and I doubt my father would prefer I inhaled a shit load of coke up my nose instead.

I give him a mock salute as he turns and saunters off into the crowd, grinning like we were just having a pleasant father-son catch up and he doesn't have a care in the world. On the far side of the room, the string quartet I saw setting up earlier begins to play, sending the glossy, warm notes of Boccherini's Minuet floating up toward the high ceiling. Such a fucking farce.

Suddenly the tie around my neck feels like it's choking me. Laura looks up from the conversation she's sharing with the young guy I don't know and gives me a small wave, beckoning me over. I don't want to go over there and be introduced to the halfwit son of one of my asshole father's Harvard buddies. I'd rather poke my eyes out with a shitty stick than do the whole run of the mill, *yes, I went to MIT. No, I don't know so-and-so. Yes, I served in the military. No, I won't tell you the most fucked up thing I ever saw. No, I won't tell you how many people I killed, you fucking tourist* bit. Still, it would seem I have very little choice in the matter. Laura grins at me as I weave my way toward her.

"Jamie!" She throws her arm around my waist, inserting herself into

4

the space at my side so that I naturally put my arm around her shoulders. She looks up at me with those big, brown eyes of hers and winks. "Jamie, this is Edward Lamont. He's the son of one of your father's friends. They…" She frowns, turning back to Edward. "How does your father know the governor again?"

"Oh, they went to college together."

Well, color me motherfucking surprised.

Edward holds his hand out to me, a wall of white, glow-in-the-dark teeth almost blinding me as he sends a smile my way. "Pleased to meet you, Jamie. I've heard a lot about you. Your father is an incredible man."

"Isn't he just?" I pump Over Eager Eddie's hand firmly just the once and turn my full attention on Laura. "Where's your brother, anyway? I haven't seen him yet."

"Oh, he's here somewhere. I think Daddy was showing him off to the head of some private security firm or something. Hey, you're not going, are you?" She has that kicked puppy thing going on as I disentangle myself from her embrace. I know she was trying to use me as a shield between her and Edward, but I really don't have the energy to play nice at the moment.

"Sorry, Lore. I'll be back soon, I promise. Edward, it was a pleasure to make your acquaintance." Laura shoots daggers at me as I duck off into the confusion of people. I'll probably be hearing about it for weeks, but I had to bail. No two ways about it. I can't find Cade in amongst the sea of dusty, gray-haired old fucks and their plastic, bleach blonde wives, so I grab a whiskey from Sarah, ask her how her new grandbaby is, and quietly go about getting drunk alone in a dark corner.

My father moves from one small group of people to the next, continually shoveling canapés into his mouth and pouring champagne down his throat until he's tripping over his own damned size tens. Looks like this year's speech is going to be slurred again. Eventually the quartet stop playing and take a break, and I spy Cade on the other side of the room, talking to Laura and Over Eager Eddie. No way am I going over there now. I've had six whiskeys and I already successfully escaped that clusterfuck once. Cade will come find me when he's had enough of this pretentious bullshit, by which point I will be comfortably numb, anyway.

"Excuse me? Do you...? Hi. Do you know where the bathrooms are? I'm dying over here and I only have a few minutes." In front of me, a petite little brunette with pretty cornflower blue eyes is clasping her hands in front of her stomach, looking like she's about to pee on my father's highly polished parquet. The short black dress she's wearing shows off her tanned, rather delectable legs.

"Do I know where the bathroom is?" I ask.

"Yes. I'm sorry, you probably don't have a clue either," she says, laughing nervously.

"Oh, I know where they are. I grew up here." I sling back the last of the whiskey in my glass and slowly place the tumbler at my feet. I offer her my arm. "Come on. I will escort you there directly."

She looks up at me like a frightened baby deer, her cheeks flushing, but she places her hand into the crook of my arm and follows me all the same. I don't take her to the downstairs bathroom behind the staircase. I don't take her to the one through the servants' walkway, just next to the kitchen. I lead her up to the next floor, straight to the en suite of one of father's overly plain guest bedrooms.

"Thank you. If you go back downstairs and see a really stressed out looking violinist, will you let him know I won't be a second?"

I lean against the wall, pulling roughly at my tie. "You're one of the musicians, then?"

Her cheeks turn crimson. "Yes. I'm...the cellist."

I have a very witty response lined up about her liking a solid piece of wood between her legs, but I keep my mouth shut. She's not the sort of girl you use that kind of innuendo on. She is the kind of girl you tread carefully with. I'm not one for the softly, softly approach, though. There's a fine line between terrifying a woman like this and getting her so wound up that she's trembling at the knees.

"You're very beautiful. Do you know that?"

She swallows. "I—thank you. That's very kind of you."

"Do you think I'm attractive?"

"What?"

"Do you think I'm attractive?"

"Well, that's not a question people normally ask you five seconds after meeting," she says, laughing softly.

"Maybe not. But you're here, working, and I'm here, suffering, and it seems to me that both of us are going to be leaving this place soon. We're probably never going to see each other again. So we don't have much time to waste. If you don't think I'm attractive, I'll happily be a gentleman and go back downstairs. Is that what you want?"

She looks at me like I just told her aliens are invading and the planet is about to be blown to smithereens. Her mouth opens and then closes twice. "I—"

"Don't worry, little cellist. I'll go find your stressed violinist and tell him you'll be down in a second." I make to leave, but she places a hand on my arm, stopping me in my tracks.

"Of course I think you're hot," she says quietly. "You're, like, a young, sexy James Bond in that suit. And your eyes are..." She shakes her head, apparently not sure how to finish that sentence. "Maybe I do want you to be here when I come out of the bathroom. Is that bad?"

Leaning down so that my mouth's mere inches away from hers, I stare at her lips, knowing she wants me to kiss her. Knowing she wants me to do any number of very bad things to her. "Go use the bathroom. When you come out, I'll show you just how bad we can be together."

Her breath catches in her throat, but she doesn't change her mind. She does as she's told and uses the bathroom, and when she comes out I make good on my words.

At the precise moment Laura bursts into the room calling out my name, I have my tongue down the little cellist's throat, her dress pulled down to her waist exposing her breasts, and two of my fingers inside her wet pussy.

Laura screeches to a halt, a horrified look spreading across her face. *"Jesus, Jamie."*

"Oh my god." The little cellist scrambles back into her clothing, hanging her head as she wriggles away from me. "Oh my god, I am *so* sorry."

"You have nothing to apologize for," I tell her, but she's moving so frantically that she can't hear me. Laura watches her hurry out of the room with her mouth hanging open like a swinging trapdoor. I'm still completely dressed, and thanks to Laura's untimely entrance my hard-on has completely vanished, too. "Perfect, Lore. Just fucking perfect. Have you forgotten how to knock?"

"Are you *kidding* me?" She throws her hands up in the air, staring at me in disbelief. "You're the one up here finger fucking some twenty-one-year old, and you're giving *me* shit?"

It's kind of hilarious to hear Laura say *finger fucking*, but I manage to keep the smile from my face. "What's wrong? You never been caught in flagrante before, Laura Preston? Never been caught with your panties down?"

"No!" She looks like she's lost for a second, and then she's kicking off her monstrous golden skyscraper heels and she's, shit, she's *throwing* them at me.

The first heel misses me by a mile. The second one buzzes my head and hits the huge gilt-framed mirror hanging on the wall behind me, smashing the glass into a million tiny pieces. "*What the fuck, Laura?*"

"You! I can't..." She clasps her hand over her mouth and that's when I notice her eyes are filled with tears. "I can't fucking believe you," she whispers.

Oh, crap. This is not how someone reacts to busting their friend doing something questionable. This is not how they react at all. I cross the room, holding up my hands as I approach her, stooping slightly so I can look her in the eye. "Hey. *Hey.* I'm really fucking confused. Do you want to tell me what's wrong, or should I go get Cade?"

"Don't you dare go and fucking get Cade," she hisses. "You and Cade, joined at the hip, twenty-four fucking seven. You and Cade vanishing off to fucking Afghanistan, leaving me here on my own. I waited here for you for four goddamn years, Jamie. Four years of waking up every single night in a cold sweat, wondering which one of you was going to die first. And then you come home and hardly even...hardly even look at me and..."

Oh.

Fuck.

Seriously?

Her hair, perfectly pinned back when she came charging into the room, has now come loose and is tumbling into her face like it used to when she was a little girl. I reach out, tucking it behind her ear. "Laura—"

"No. Don't! Fuck, Jamie, you just had your fingers inside some girl's vagina."

I consider pointing out that that was my other hand, but then come to the swift conclusion that Laura will probably strangle me to death with my own necktie if I do. I slide my hands inside my pockets, clearing my throat. "Lore," I say carefully. "Is there something you wanna tell me?"

"Fuck you, Jamie. I shouldn't have to tell you. You should already know! Ahhh! Men! Why are you all so fucking oblivious? How can you be that completely blind to what's been staring you in the face since we were kids, Jay. I just...I gotta get out of here."

She's a whirlwind of tense energy and clenched fists as she storms out of the bedroom. I go after her, grabbing hold of her gently by the wrist, trying to stop her, trying to figure this whole thing out in my head fast enough to deal with it right here and now, but Laura has other ideas. She turns on me, hand raised, and her palm makes contact with my face, slapping me hard. I can see from the pain in her eyes that she regrets it immediately.

"*Shit.*" She covers her mouth with her hand. "Shit, I'm so sorry. I just—"

"It's okay."

"I just can't—" Tears roll, round and fat, down her cheeks, dangling like tiny little crystals from her dark eyelashes.

"It's okay," I repeat. "It's fine. We can talk about it tomorrow."

She nods, just once. "Tomorrow," she says. And then she goes, running down the sweeping staircase in her bare feet, tiny sparks of light bouncing everywhere like silent fireworks as the sequins of her dress catch the light.

It's not until the next morning that Cade calls to tell me his sister never made it home.

REBEL

War isn't always a loud, brash thing.

Sometimes, it's a car rolling slowly by the front of your house at night. Sometimes, it's an anonymous call to the police. Sometimes it's the head of a Mexican cartel showing up in small town New Mexico to make your life a living hell. And sometimes, it's three men sneaking through tall grass with guns in their hands, ready to shoot you in the head while you sleep.

I'm bleeding fucking everywhere. One of Hector Ramirez's perimeter guards cut me open with his knife and now the wound is pouring my DNA out all over the grass. I can't be thinking about that right now, though. Honestly, I'm not thinking at all. I'm gripped with the same insanity that's had hold of me since I walked into my father's kitchen and found Leah dead on the floor, her throat slit from ear to ear, and that smug motherfucker toasting me from the other side of the room. There's no room for sanity inside me now. Not after Leah. My uncle was one thing, but add on another innocent woman who I was supposed to be protecting, and there is no more Jamie. Even Rebel doesn't exist anymore. There is only madness and fury, held together with the burning acid of revenge. It's eaten away at everything else until there's nothing left.

I feel a hand on the center of my back, grabbing hold of my t-shirt. It's Cade, trying to tell me to slow the fuck down, but I jerk myself away, hurrying forward. Behind me, I hear him cursing me to hell. Carnie's back there somewhere, too. Just the three of us for this job. As the newest member of the Widow Makers, I shouldn't have brought Carnie along on this particular ride, but the guy's keen as fuck. He totally busted Cade and me as we were leaving the compound. He would have followed us here, regardless. He's had Margo, the gun he named after his mother, locked and loaded ever since he climbed on his Ducati.

The very day after Sophia and I returned from Alabama, Hector showed up with his entourage, walking the streets like he owns the fucking place, drinking coffee outside *my* fucking tattoo shop, sending out a very clear message: *I am here to end this.* And if that's what the guy wants, who am I to argue with him?

I've had enough. I should have sent Sophia away the second I saw that body in my father's kitchen and I realized this thing was never going to make it to trial. Never going to make it past pure, old school, *knife-in-the-chest-while-you're-sleeping* revenge. Soph should be at home with her family, and instead I have her under guard back in my cabin, probably tearing the place apart, raging mad, and all because I've put her in this shitty position. Because where Hector Ramirez goes, so follows Raphael Dela Vega. And after what Sophia told me—that Raphael threatened to kill her whole family and do way worse to her— I'm not letting her out of that cabin until the fucker is dead and in the ground.

"Dude, slow the fuck down. They're gonna see us coming," Cade hisses behind me. Up ahead, the ground floor of the small, innocuous farm house Hector's taken up residence in is lit up against the darkness, pouring yellowed light out onto the wrap around porch that skirts the property. Shadows move inside. I didn't really think for a second I was going to be rolling up on a sleeping house but it's frustrating that there are so many people flitting from room to room. I'm only interested in killing one person: Hector.

After Afghanistan, I have enough blood on my hands to drown myself in. I don't particularly want to add to the body count, but if they stand in my way, if killing them means I get to put an end to Ramirez, then so be it. My soul is already damned to hell. I might as well *really* earn my place there.

The night smells like gasoline and bad weed, the latter of which must be coming from the house. Crouching down low thirty meters from the illuminated building, I scan the darkness, trying to see if there are more watchmen that need putting down. I made a stupid, reckless error before. I wasn't expecting there to be guards so far out on the very perimeters of the farmhouse. When the first guy emerged out of the black night and slashed at me, he took me by surprise. Between me, Cade and Carnie, we managed to put down the four men who rallied to take us on, but it was close. Stupid. I should have been more wary. I'm not just risking my own life here, but Cade and Carnie's too.

"How many?" Cade whispers. My best friend scratches at the beard he's managed to grow in the past few weeks, frowning severely. I can't count how many times we've found ourselves together in this position, crouching in the dark, planning on doing wrong. It's little comfort that the majority of times it was on behalf of the U.S government. We may not be desert rats anymore, but we're still soldiers. We're still fighting a war. Except this is one of our own making, and there's no getting out of it. No backing down. It's *necessary*.

"At least six," I reply.

"I only count five," Carnie chips in. "Three in the living room, one in the kitchen. One in the hallway."

He's right, but his eyes aren't as sharp as mine. I glare up at the farmhouse, holding my breath, slowing my pulse. "And one more. Upstairs. Front left window. He's watching us right now."

Carnie makes a disbelieving sound. "You're fucking crazy. The room's pitch black. You can't see shit."

"Oh, he's there all right. I can see him just fine." In fairness to Carnie, maybe I can't see him in a traditional sense. The room *is* in pure darkness, but I can sense it—Ramirez is there, standing in the murky shadows of the room, waiting patiently for my arrival. I can feel his presence so intensely that the hairs on the back of my neck are standing on end. He's been there all along, just waiting for me to show up. With all the showmanship and blatant peacocking in town, he's been stabbing at my buttons, knowing that with each and every sighting he's coming closer and closer to drawing me out.

I'm a stupid motherfucker.

I'm normally so much smarter than this, but the fury over Ryan and Leah's deaths has had me taking temporary leave of my wits. Cade nudges me with his elbow, grunting softly. "We're here, man. You wanna do this now, we'll do it. But maybe—"

"Yeah, I know." I sigh heavily. Angrily. I want to pound my fists into the dirt in frustration, but where the fuck would that get me.

"You might be wrong," Carnie whispers. "I get bad feelings all the time. Your brain plays some epic tricks on you sometimes."

"He's not wrong, asshole. He's never been wrong." The dull thump of Cade punching Carnie in the arm is quiet, but Carnie's yelp of pain isn't. "Jesus, man. Shut your fucking mouth. You wanna get us killed?"

"I don't think he's seen us," I whisper, ignoring them. "But I can't be sure. Time to leave." Leaving is the very last thing I want to do. I want to storm into that building and shoot some motherfuckers. I want to dig the point of my blade into Hector Ramirez's chest and watch the light go out in his eyes as the steel bites deeper. But Ramirez is a smart guy. He knows I'm coming. There's no way there's only six people in that building. He will have an army of men hidden out of sight, ready to end our lives before we even step foot on the fucking farmhouse porch.

"Come on, man. We'll get the fucker, don't you worry. But this ain't how it goes down," Cade says. I let him pull me back, let his words deaden the boiling adrenalin storming my veins, calling for revenge. I suddenly feel exhausted.

"All right. All right," I take a deep breath, uncurling my hands, not realizing they were clenched into fists. As I retreat from the farmhouse with my boys, ducking low to remain out of sight, I feel sick to my stomach. We're leaving with our lives, but somehow it feels like a defeat. I'm chanting the same words over and over as the farmhouse shrinks and disappears behind us.

This isn't over, motherfucker. It's only just begun.

SOPHIA

I've given up screaming. It didn't get me anywhere for two days so I figured why waste the energy. I haven't seen Rebel in ten days. Ten days couped up in his cabin while he's out there doing god knows what and I've been going bat shit crazy. I thought we were past this. I thought this part was over. I should have known by his silent, brooding mood on the way back from Alabama that things were right back to where we were in the beginning. More fool me for assuming that me agreeing to help him, me turning down the opportunity to flee back to my family, me *fucking him* for fuck's sake, would change things between us. Now, I just feel foolish. For all of it.

There *was* a brief moment where I did get to step outside. Seventy two hours after Rebel put the Humvee in park and bundled me into his house on the hill, locking the door behind me, the prospect, Carnie, showed up and drove me out into the desert, kicking and screaming. He wouldn't tell me why at first, but after an hour of me chewing his ear off, threatening to scream blue murder the whole time we were sitting in his shitty, beaten up Firebird, the guy caved.

"The cops are tearing the compound apart, looking for evidence to link the club to that shooting in Los Angeles."

I'm horrified when it takes me a beat to remember what he's talking about—the shooting at Trader Joes, where all those civilians were killed by men wearing Widow Makers cuts.

"Yeah, one of Rebel's uncle's friends called and gave him a heads up. Told Rebel the police caught the guys who did it in Irvine, still wearing the fake cuts, drunk as all hell. The fat one who was supposed to be the club president confessed that they'd been hired for the job. Gave up Maria Rosa in a heart beat, in exchange for a lesser sentence."

"Is she still going to cause problems then? This Maria Rosa?"

Carnie gets a far away look in his eye that looks almost romantic. "From what I've been told, the Bitch of Columbia causes problems wherever she is in the world. I wouldn't be surprised."

He drove me back to the compound at nightfall and took me straight back to the cabin, ignoring my colorful language and my threats to take him out at the knees.

That was last Wednesday. Now it's Wednesday again. Tomorrow morning I should be getting up at seven and going for a run before heading to my Human Sciences class. Instead, Carnie, with his busted up glasses and his hipster side-parting will bring me my breakfast and refuse to tell me anything, and I'll swear at him or completely blank him depending on my mood. The cycle repeats itself endlessly, over and over.

Tonight, however, Carnie's already dropped off my evening meal. I called him a soulless bastard and threw the plate of meatloaf at his head, but the thing missed him entirely and impacted with the wall. I need to do some serious work on my aim. The meatloaf has sat on the floor since then, getting colder and staler by the second, in amongst the shattered shards of the chinaware.

If Sloane were here she would have figured out how to free herself from this fucked up situation. I can guarantee it. She's resourceful, independent and stubborn, and she wouldn't give up until she found a way to get what she wanted. That makes me even madder as I sit and watch The Hangover for the eighteenth time. The TV in Rebel's cabin has no reception, just a handful of DVDs, all of which are the same kind of stupid, mindless humor I would never normally watch. Now, I've seen every single last one of them. I'm beginning to know them line for line.

Alan is just confessing that he drugged the other guys in the movie when the door to the cabin flies open and Rebel stalks in, larger than life. It's the last thing I'm expecting, given that I've been asking to see him for the past week and a half and he hasn't graced me with his presence. A part of me got to thinking that maybe he was hurt or something. Injured, to the point where he was laid up and incapable of walking. Standing in the doorway now, I can see that he's walking just fine. He glances down at his feet and scowls at the debris from my evening meal on the floorboards.

"What the fuck?" He looks at me like I'm a naughty child, caught misbehaving, and I automatically shrink back into the sofa. I catch myself, almost screaming out loud at how ridiculous my reaction is. I shouldn't be shrinking from him. I'm a fucking prisoner. I'm allowed to revolt if I damn well want to. "Got a problem?" I snap, sitting up straighter.

"Yeah. There's fucking food all over my damn floor. I hand-sanded these floorboards," he growls.

"Then you should have thrown me in the basement or something and had done with it, shouldn't you?"

"Don't fucking tempt me." Rebel steps over the mess and slams the door behind him, locking it before he storms into the room. I try not to flinch as he comes to a stop in front of me. "Stand up, Soph."

I take a deep breath. "*No.*" My skin feels tingly, the same way it used to when I would defy my father. Not that I'm comparing the man standing in front of me with the mild mannered preacher left worrying about me back in Seattle, but this situation feels...it feels very much like I'm about to get punished.

Tilting his head to one side, Rebel drops into a crouch so that our eyes are at the same level. His are ice-blue, cold. Intense. So fierce I can hardly meet them. I'm proud of the fact that I don't look away, though. "What seems to be the problem?" He asks this slowly, as though he's wrestling with his temper.

Had a bad night, buddy? Well guess what? So have I. Leaning forward so my face is closer to his, I breathe deep and even down my nose, trying to tame my own anger. "You're fucking kidding me, right?"

He blinks. He's frozen solid, staring straight at me. He's holding himself back, but from what I'm not entirely sure. Not for a second do I think he's going to hurt me, but there's something about the brooding, stillness of him that's intimidating. "Have you been bored or something?"

"You could say that."

"You know what's not boring?" Calm. He's too fucking calm. It's beginning to put me on edge. He continues speaking softly, but there's a dangerous lilt to his voice. "Being chased down, raped and murdered. That's not boring, right?"

"This place is a fortress, Jamie. I would have been fine out there with everyone else. How many people do you have living at the compound for crying out loud? There must be twenty motorcycles here at any one time!"

He cocks his head again, frowning. He's probably wondering how I know that; you can see nothing but trees and then a distant ridgeline from the cabin windows. With so little to do all day, I've gotten really good at listening, though. I knew nothing about engines before I came here. I don't really know anything about them now, either, apart from the fact that each one sounds different. I've spent hours laying on Rebel's bed with my eyes closed, listening hard. Figuring out which motorcycle was which. Who was coming and going. Not knowing who was riding what, of course, but still.

Rebel's eyes flash, the muscles in his jaw jumping as he grinds his teeth. "Raphael Dela Vega's here. In town."

"Wait. *What*?" My arms and legs suddenly feel very cold, very numb. That...that makes no sense. What would he be doing here? My anger towards Rebel doesn't matter anymore. Bile rises up in the back of my throat as I try to process this piece of information, but it's as though it just won't settle in my mind. New Mexico is so far removed from Seattle, and so very far removed from Los Angeles. My brain tries to scramble, to come up with some logical reason why Raphael would be here, here of all places. Some reason other than the fact that he must have come for me. I draw a blank.

Rebel shifts for the first time, wincing a little, like he's in pain. "I don't even want him to *see* you here, Sophia. If he does, he'll likely try and find a way into the compound, and then what? Someone's back's turned and you're lying in a pool of your own goddamn blood? No. No way." He says this so quietly, and yet there's such determination behind his words.

"You haven't been by here in ten days," I growl.

He blinks again, staring straight at me. "Would you have wanted to see me?"

"Yes! I sure as hell wouldn't want to be kept in the dark over what's going on in the outside world! You...*we slept together!* And then you're just gone. You lock me up and then you just vanish off the face of the earth."

"So that's it? You just wanted someone to come fuck you? I'm sure any of the boys would have obliged you if only you'd have told them."

I react without thinking. I'm lunging at him, my hand flying out to strike him across the face before I can stop myself. My palm makes contact with his cheek, a loud cracking sound filling the room. "Don't you fucking dare," I grind out. "Don't you dare do that. You fucking buy me like I'm nothing but a lump of meat, like I'm goddamn *property*, and then you make me care about you. You make me think you care about me. You trick me, make me look like an absolute idiot, and then you try and make me out to be some sort of slut, too. Don't you fucking *dare*."

My whole body is vibrating with anger. I've heard the saying 'seeing red' before and I've thought nothing of it, but now I know it's actually a very literal term—it's almost as though I'm seeing him through a red haze.

Rebel runs his tongue over his teeth, slowly lifting his hand to touch his fingers to the red welt on his face where I struck him. He speaks carefully, very slowly. "Sophia, please know, you're just about the only person on the face of the planet who could get away with that right now."

"Yeah? Well, if you don't get the hell away from me, I'm gonna do it again, asshole," I spit.

"I went out with the intention of killing a man tonight. You think I'll have any moral objection to tying up a misbehaving woman?"

I lean forward even further so that our faces are no less than an inch apart. "*Try me.*"

Rebel's calm, overly controlled behavior should have clued me into the fact that he's been on the verge of snapping this whole time. He rockets forward, hands grabbing me by the tops of my arms, pinning me to the sofa. "You really don't want to do this with me, Soph," he breathes.

I do, though. I want to gouge his eyes out. I want to smash my fist into his face so hard that he loses teeth. I want to break his bones and watch him bleed. I think maybe he expected me to back down as soon as he grabbed hold of me, but I don't. I twist underneath him, slamming my knee into his side. He doubles over, huffing out a deep, pained breath. Wrenching my arms out of his grasp, I slip out from underneath him and drive my clenched fist into his side as hard as I possibly can. Rebel grits his teeth, snarling between them, jumping to his feet.

"You're fucking crazy!"

"I guess that's what happens to a person when you lock them away for ten days on their own, and then show up accusing them of being a whore."

"I didn't accuse you of being a whore."

"You may as well have done. You think just because I slept with you, I'd want to sleep with any of your gross, Neanderthal groupies? I'm not some club hooker to be passed around like a damn party favor!"

He comes at me again, reaching for me, and that's when I notice the blood on his hands. My mind instantly rewinds to what he just said about setting out to kill someone tonight, and I reel back. Oh my god. No, he couldn't have. Did...*did he actually do it?* Rebel sees my anger change to horror and swiftly stops in his tracks.

"What?"

"Your hands, Rebel. What the fuck is all over your hands?"

He looks down at them, a small frown creasing his forehead, eyebrows banking together. The expression he's wearing screams innocent confusion, however the wet blood on his hands screams something else entirely. His face is ashen.

"I don't..."

I scream when he staggers sideways and crashes into the couch, dropping to one knee. "What the hell? Rebel? *Rebel*!" He looks like he's on death door. "Oh, god, please...what's wrong?" I touch his side, the side I rammed with my knee, my hand comes away covered in blood. His t-shirt is drenched with it. I didn't notice before since the material is black, but now that I'm looking closer I can see the dark, wet stain spreading across his stomach.

"Is this...is this *you*?"

Rebel nods, holding one hand to his side. "Go and get Cade."

"What happened?"

"Go and get Cade, Soph."

"Rebel!"

"Jesus, I was stabbed earlier. You just kneed me right on top of the wound. Now, please, fuck...go and get Cade."

I'm not going anywhere. I drop to my knees beside him, tearing at his shirt. "Show me. Show me for god's sake." The bastard deserves to be in pain after everything he's put me through since we returned to New Mexico, but now that he's potentially bleeding out on the floor of his cabin, I'm suddenly not so sure that I want him to die.

He tries to pull shirt back down, but ironically I'm stronger than him right now. A jolt of surprise hits me when I see what's underneath—a seven-inch long gash runs down his ribcage, onto his stomach. And it's seriously deep. "*Are you insane? Why the hell didn't you go straight to the hospital?*" Yelling at him probably isn't the most constructive thing I could be doing, but it's about all I can think of. Rebel grimaces, slumping back so that he's sitting on his ass on the floor.

"It wasn't bleeding that much before you belted me," he says. Unbelievably, he winks at me, like he finds that highly amusing.

"Shit. I'm sorry. I am *so* sorry. God, I need to find a towel." I start pacing, tearing through drawers and cupboards, searching but not finding what I'm looking for.

"It's okay, it's all right. I don't need a towel. Soph. *Sophia!*"

I stop pacing.

"Go and get Cade, okay? He'll be up in the bar, in the biggest building. Go and get him and tell him to bring a suture kit." Rebel reaches up and hands me a key, and it takes me a second to understand what it's for: the door to the cabin. The door to my freedom. I take it from him.

There's an actual pool of blood spreading out around him on the floorboards now, growing bigger by the second. I did that to him. Well, I didn't do it to him, but I sure as hell made it worse. *Fuck.* I run to the door and unlock it, my hands shaking like crazy., and then I'm running some more, running to the left toward a building I've only ever seen from a distance as I've been brought to and from the cabin. Tall, dead grass whips at my bare legs as I barrel head on down the steep hill that leads to the rest of the compound. The night air feels cool in my lungs, pulling at my clothes as I sprint for help.

It occurs to me that I could veer to the right, towards the banks of motorcycles and cars parked off the side. I have no idea how to hot wire a car but I could give it a damn good go. A part of my brain is screaming at me to do it, to let Rebel bleed out on the floor, steal a car and head for the closest police station, but I can't. I just can't make myself do it. Rebel was a major asshole when he came back to the cabin just now, but I saw something in him in Alabama. Something that made me drop my defences and trust him. I can't just let him die.

When I slam though the doors of the main building, I see it must be the Widow Makers' clubhouse. Inside, at least fifteen people stop their conversations, glasses and beer bottles held halfway to their mouths, and they all turn to stare at me. A tall woman, maybe in her late forties cocks her head to one side and blinks like she can't believe what she's seeing. Cade's on the other side of the room, paused mid-hand shake with another, shorter guy with neck tattoos. His eyes nearly pop out of his head when he sees me.

"What in Sam Hell?" Cade drops his friend's hand and storms across the clubhouse bar, murder in his eyes. "You trying to get yourself killed?" he hisses, grabbing hold of my arm. I've had enough of people manhandling me for one day. Ripping my arm free, I step back, ready to knee him somewhere a little more intimate if I have to.

"Rebel needs you. He said for you to bring a suture kit," I tell him. If I were my sister, I could have sewn Rebel up myself. I'm not though, so this is the best I can do. I shove Cade in the chest, trying to transfer some sense of urgency to him. "He's bleeding everywhere," I snap. "When he sent me to fetch you, I don't think he had a huge amount of time for you to decide if you were gonna come or not."

Cade scrubs his hand with his face, rolling his eyes. "Jesus, I told him he should go see the doc." He ducks quickly behind the bar, where an overweight guy in an ACDC t-shirt is staring at me with eyes like saucers. It takes me a moment to realize why: I'm half freaking naked. It may be winter, but you wouldn't know it by the temperature in New Mexico. I've been sweltering in Rebel's airless, AC-less cabin. Shorts and tank tops have been my recent staple.

The fact that my shirt is covered in blood really isn't helping matters, either. I try to shrink inside my own skin as Cade grabs a small green case from somewhere underneath the counter, and then he's vaulting over it and leading me out of the bar. I glance over my shoulder just in time to catch the hateful look being sent my way by a beautiful pink haired woman with tattoos. Her eyes narrow at me, and then she's gone as I'm dragged out of the clubhouse and across the compound in the direction of the cabin.

"Is he conscious?" Cade asks.

"Was when I left him," I pant. "There was blood on the floor, though. A lot of blood."

Cade just grunts. He lets me go and takes off without a backward glance to make sure I'm following. Again, I'm presented with the opportunity to escape. Rebel is about to get help. Cade will either stitch him up or take him to get further medical attention. My usefulness in this situation is at an end. I should be ducking into the shadows and vanishing, even if I can't get one of the cars to work and I have to walk to the next town.

I take a deep breath, watching Cade growing smaller and smaller as he runs up the hill to Rebel's place, and then I'm looking over my shoulder, out over the endless, scrubby desert between me and civilization...and I'm shaking my head.

I could die out there. That's not what stops me from running, though. It's the fact that Rebel could die right here, right now and I would never know it.

My head is swimming as I run up the hill behind Cade. I've lost my mind. I must be completely insane to be doing this. My father's face flashes through my head as I summit the hill, running directly back *into* the place I've been desperate to escape from the past ten days. In my head, for some weird reason, my father is smiling.

REBEL

I can't remember the last time I threw up. Certainly not for any reason other than being blind fucking drunk, anyway. I mean, yes, I suppose I do feel really drunk, but that's because I'm losing copious amounts of blood and I can't seem to stem the flow. I'm retching, head spinning, vision blurred when I see a dark shape coming toward me. Coming toward me fast.

"Fuck me, man, what the hell?" It's Cade. His voice reaches me, though it sounds muffled, like I've got cotton wool stuffed inside my ears. "Well, aren't you in a state."

I weakly lift my right hand from the ground and flip him off. Cade laughs. "See why you sent for me now, jackass," he says. "Guy gives you a couple of pints of blood in a foreign country and the next thing you know it's five years later an' he wants the damn stuff back. *Indian giver.*" He laughs under his breath, and my brain works sluggishly, trying to decipher what he's talking about .

Ah, yeah. That's right. Afghanistan. We were in Afghanistan and he was shot. He'd lost a lot of blood. I gave him some of mine. The doctors performed a transfusion because we were the same blood type, and Cade was my brother and I wouldn't just sit by and watch him die while we waited around for the bagged stuff to arrive.

I've been fighting to stay upright, to stay awake, but now that he's here, I feel like I can stop fighting so hard. The bastard won't let me die, I know it. I fall back, my head bouncing off the floor, and then Cade's hands are on my torso, spinning me over slowly so that I'm on my side.

Pain washes through me, like I'm being stabbed all over again. It's weird, though, the ghost of what pain should really feel like. Everything's going numb. That's how it starts…dying. Your nerve endings start playing tricks on you, cutting your brain off from your limbs or making you think you're really cold. At this particular point in time, I feel like I'm half frozen.

"Better…hurry your…ass up," I stutter. It's shock. I know it is. My whole body is starting to shake.

Another voice speaks, catching at my focus for a second. Sophia. My hands involuntarily twitch, my fingers curling inwards, as though reaching for the idea of her. "What…what should I do?" she asks.

I can't see her, but I can sense her close. "Hold this," Cade tells her. I can't see what he hands her. She's standing behind me, breathing quickly, like she's hyperventilating. Pain bites through me, a sudden, sharp reminder of how shitty it is when your nerve endings actually decide to work in situations like this. Carefully, slowly, I look down, struggling to focus my eyes on what's happening to my chest. Cade is quickly, efficiently stitching me back together, my skin tugging and pulling as he forcefully shoves the needle in and out of my skin.

"Any…internal…?" I manage.

"No. No, your insides are just fine, you lucky son of a bitch, now hold still."

I hold still, grinding my teeth together as I'm put back together. I manage to stay awake until the very final stitch is tied off, and then I pass the fuck out.

I could be out for hours, but I get the feeling it's more like fifteen minutes. When I regain consciousness, Cade is standing over me, glaring grimly at me while he wipes his hands on one of my bathroom towels, and Sophia is sitting on the edge of the bed, wearing next to nothing. If I had any blood left in my body, I'm sure it would be headed straight for my dick right now. As it goes, I roll over slowly and throw up over the side of the bed.

"Nice," Cade observes. "Real fucking nice."

"Fuck you, man." It sounds like I've been eating gravel. My head is splitting apart. I fall back onto the pillows, my stomach rolling again, making empty threats. There can't be anything left inside me to bring back up by now. Sophia grimaces at the mess I've made; she gets to her feet and heads for the kitchen bench, rifling under the counters, presumably looking for cleaning products.

"Don't. You don't have to do that," I say, wincing.

Cade lifts an eyebrow, shaking his head. "Sure she does, man. I'm gonna sit here and let you steal half my plasma. I ain't gonna clean up your puke, too."

"Then deal with it," I growl. "She shouldn't have to—"

"I don't mind. I don't want to sit here looking at it, either." Soph drops to her knees and starts mopping up my vomit, which makes me feel about three fucking inches tall. While she's doing that, Cade sets up for the blood transfusion. He must have gone back to the clubhouse and grabbed the tourniquets, lines and needles while I was briefly out for the count.

I lay on my back with my arm thrown up over my eyes while Cade efficiently hooks us up and begins the process. It's such a strange feeling, having blood traveling *into* your body instead of out. I can hear Sophia throwing things into the trash. Can smell the disinfectant she's scrubbing into the floorboards as Cade makes underhanded comments about how fucking stupid I am.

"And by the way," he tells me. "I smoked a bunch of weed as soon as I walked through the door earlier. Don't know if that shit affects your blood, but I sure hope it fucking does. It'll serve you right if you get insanely high and pass out again. You've totally ruined my buzz."

I consider trying to punch him, but just thinking of the effort that would involve exhausts me. I decide on a different tack. "Thanks, man.

"Don't mention it."

I lay there, thinking about the ridiculous shit I said to Soph before she went postal and tried to murder me. I should have kept my mouth shut. I've been completely thrown since we got back here, though. Ten days I stayed away, because me being around her is a bad idea. Actually, no. Before, back when Ramirez didn't know exactly who I was and where my fucking family lived, it was a bad idea. Now he does know and he's shown up on my front door step, it's a fucking *catastrophic* idea. We should never have gotten involved the way we did back in Alabama. I should never have gone after her like that. What a fucking moronic thing to do.

Thirty minutes pass. I spend the entire time mentally kicking my own ass. Eventually, Cade removes the needle from the crook of my arm. "All right. We're done. Here, take this," Cade tells me. I lower my arm, eyeing the four white tablets in the palm of his hand with suspicion.

"What is it?"

"Azithromycin."

"Where did you get it?"

"Carnie had the clap last month. Said it knocked it right on the head." Cade grins as he says this, the motherfucker.

"Fantastic. Now I'm taking medication from Carnie's dick infections."

"I've given you some pretty sweet codeine in there too," Cade informs me. You're gonna feel really good in about twenty minutes."

I take the pills because I don't really feel like heading down to the local doctor's surgery and getting my own prescription of antibiotics. At this stage, I couldn't manage that anyway, even if I really did feel like answering the probing questions that come with a stab wound consultation.

Cade slips out of the cabin, leaving me on my back, staring up the ceiling, wondering what the hell I'm supposed to say to the quiet girl hovering in the corner of the room.

I'm such a complete and utter asshole. I shouldn't have even come storming back up the hill to the cabin when we got back from Ramirez's farmhouse. I should have just kept my cool and stayed on track. Stayed the fuck away. But, oh no, I had to be in a shitty mood. I had to fucking see her.

"Does it hurt?" Sophia's voice is soft, and yet it feels like a slap to the face. One I deserve, and then some. When I open my eyes, she's sitting on the floor a few feet away from the bed, like she's afraid I'm about to jump up and backhand her. Seeing the panic in her eyes makes me feel physically sick all over again.

"Not really," I lie. "Could be worse." *Yeah, I could be fucking dead.*

"You feel a bit better now?" She sounds like she's on the brink of tears. There's a defiant look on her face, but her hands are shaking. I can see the slight tremor as she twists a piece of thread over and over around her fingers. God, she's so damn beautiful. Why couldn't a dude have witnessed Ryan's murder? If she were a dude, I would *not* be having this problem. But then again, if she were a dude, Dela Vega would have murdered her on the spot after seeing what went down. She would have had absolutely no purpose to him. At least as a woman, he knew Ramirez might want to make some quick cash off her.

"I'll be fine tomorrow," I tell her. I won't be fine tomorrow. Truth be told, I'm probably going to be out of commission for days, if not weeks, because of this injury. And being out of commission's something I really can't afford to be right now.

I can't think about that, though. My head is still swimming. Keep my damn eyes open is becoming an almost impossible task, and the bed feels like it's pitching and rolling like a motherfucking sailboat.

"I could have run, y'know," Sophia whispers softly. "I could have just gone, run off into the night and left you here. I'd probably be halfway to the next city by now."

"You mean you'd probably be *vulture bait*," I say, correcting her. But I know she's right. She could have just left me to die. If she'd made a different decision when I sent her running out of here, there's no doubt about it—I would have been fucking long gone. "Thank you, Soph," I say quietly under my breath. "Thanks for not bailing on me."

Out of the corner of my eye, I can see her expression growing less worried and more irritated. "After what you said to me, I should have.

My sister would have probably finished the job if you'd have said that to her. She'd have strangled you to death before you even had *chance* to bleed out."

"Then I'm glad I didn't say it to her. And I'm sorry I said it to you. I shouldn't have. I know you wouldn't screw any of the guys."

"Then why say it? And why leave me here, trapped in this cabin for ten days, after I said I would help you in Alabama? It makes no sense. It's just damn cruel, in fact." She speaks slowly. I can tell she's still furious but she keeps her voice down now. No more shouting and screaming. No more trying to pile drive her knee straight through my ribcage. Given her reaction earlier, I feel like making a show of cowering from her, but it's probably still too early for jokes yet. Besides, I'd probably burst open my stitches if I move, and Cade will not be thrilled if I undo his handiwork. He'll probably stab me all over again.

"If my boys knew you were here, why you were here, or that Raphael is on the look out for you, they'll want to use you somehow," I explain. "They'll want to use you as bait or something to lure Ramirez out, and I'm not taking that kind of chance."

Soph rests her chin on her knees, staring up at me on the bed. "Yeah. Well, I mean, I don't want to be anywhere near Dela Vega or Ramirez again if I don't have to be." She sounds like even the prospect of running into either of those men is enough to give her nightmares. I'd be surprised if that's not actually the case.

"As soon as Raphael lays eyes on you here, Soph, that will be it. I know him. He's a sick motherfucker. He won't ever stop until he gets his hands on you."

Sophia shivers. Shakes her head, like she's trying to shake the very memory of him out of her body. "Why would Ramirez follow you here? Why would he actually search you out? I don't get it."

"We're not playing hide and seek, Soph. Neither side wants to drag this out. The longer we're at each other's throats, the longer Ramirez can't relax or conduct business without watching his back. The longer he can't smuggle his drugs into the country. The longer he can't focus on selling his women."

"And for you? What's this war going to distract you from, Rebel?" she looks dubious.

I smirk, thinking about shrugging my shoulders but then dismissing the idea as entirely not worth the accompanying pain. "The Widow Makers run guns. As an illegal trade, that's how all the syndicates think we make our money. It's how the ATF *think* but can't *prove* we make our money. In reality, the Widowers trade in information more than anything else. Information is far more valuable than gold or silver, drugs or guns. It can build or collapse an empire overnight. The only thing more reliable for bringing a dangerous man to his knees is pussy. And, as you're already aware, we don't sell *that*."

"No," she says, giving me a wry glance. "You only *buy* it."

"If *I* don't, someone else will. Difference being is that I find secure, honest, healthy work for the women we pay for. They leave this compound untouched. If Julio had bought you for himself, guaranteed you'd have already been accosted more times than you could count, and by more men than you could count, too. Would you have preferred that?"

Sophia remains silent. She glares at me like she hates me, but maybe, just *maybe*, like she's also considering that I may have done her a favor. Doesn't look like she'll be admitting that any time soon, though. I pull in a deep breath, testing out how deeply I can fill my lungs without experiencing any sharp, crippling pain.

"Ramirez is here because he's making his first move. He's being reckless. Perhaps I need to be, too."

"I think it's a little late for that, right?" Soph eyes my blood-covered torso with what looks like regret. "I'm really sorry. I had no idea you were hurt. You know that, right? I would never have—"

"Stop. I deserved it. We're all good."

"Still. Launching myself at you like that—

"Is part of the reason why I like you, Sophia. That fiery temper of yours is insanely hot. You looked like some wild Amazon, ready to skin me alive. I was halfway to a boner before you nearly killed me."

Sophia ducks her head, eyes skating over the floorboards, not looking at me. If I didn't know better, I'd say she was embarrassed. "Maybe you *should* use me as bait," she says abruptly. "At least that way, if my presence is somehow a catalyst for drawing Ramirez and Raphael out, then this can all be over. We could all go back to living our lives."

Laughter itches at the back of my throat. Scathing, ironic laughter. I swallow it back down. See, the thing Sophia doesn't quite realize yet is that this *is* my life. When this is all over, if I'm not dead, there will always be someone else to contend with someone else to put down. Someone else who will want to take what is ours.

I can't tell her that, though. She'll run for the hills, and despite my previous pathetic attempt at doing the right thing, I know now that it's just not possible. I have plans for the girl sitting crossed legged on the floor by my bed. Big, awesome, scary plans. I'm going to keep my mouth shut about those, too, though. Right now, there's only one thing I need to tell her.

"I'm not endangering you with those men again, Sophia. No way. Not happening. There are a lot of things I'll risk to end this. I'll risk my own life, and the lives of my club members, if they're stupid enough to volunteer them. I'll risk my freedom and every last cent I own. I'll risk the sun and the moon, and the wind on my face. But not you, Soph. I'll never risk *you*."

SOPHIA

I don't know what to make of this crazy, infuriating, ridiculously hot man. He drives me absolutely insane. One minute he's inside me in a corridor at his father's house, the next I'm being shoved back into his cabin and I'm shut away for 10 days. The man doesn't even speak to me. I don't see his face. I receive no word from him whatsoever. And now, it seems as though he's back in my life again, albeit bloody, bleeding and broken, and I don't know what to make of it.

The sun is pouring through the cabin windows, casting long shadows across the room, highlighting the dust motes swirling through the air overhead as I sleep on the bed beside Rebel. I didn't want to climb into bed with him, but the only other option was the couch and I've been uncomfortable and miserable for long enough now. Why the hell should I have to crash out on the couch? Besides, he's hardly in a position to do anything untoward at this point. The guy was practically dead last night.

It can only be about six in the morning. Already though, I can hear motorcycles arriving and leaving the compound, the brisk snarl of engines startling the birds from the trees surrounding the cabin. I'm surprised it doesn't wake Rebel up. Mind you, he appears to be sleeping the sleep of the dead. No matter how hard I try, *I* can't seem to accomplish the same feat.

I had unwelcome dreams last night. I know it's messed up, but I haven't thought about Matt since the moment I decided to give myself over to Rebel back in Alabama. I spent the last year dating a guy and I haven't thought about him once. How crazy must I be? Matt was never as thrilling or exciting as Rebel, but he was nice-looking guy, made me laugh. He was *safe*. I feel like I'm doing him a disservice by completely forgetting about him like this. I mean, who does that?

"You look like you're plotting out the world's end." I nearly jump out of my skin when I realize that Rebel *is* awake, and he's actually looking at me, frown lines marking his forehead. Sleep still hangs over him, his gaze slightly fuzzy

"Not exactly," I say. "Just wondering where we go from here?" That seems like the most practical thing to be thinking. It's no longer the sense of limbo that I find frustrating. It's the feeling of complete and utter uselessness. Ever since I saw his uncle Ryan being murdered, I've felt vulnerable and unsafe. I haven't had purpose or place in the world I've found myself in. I've been drifting, cut free from all tasks and activities that might give me some sort of mental stimulus. I've just been afraid and powerless, and that, perhaps, has been the worst part. With nothing to occupy my mind with other than my present situation, I've been driving myself crazy. At least if I know what Rebel's plan of action is, I can maybe help. Maybe I can be a part of the process. I'm kind of stunned by the intensity of his refusal to let me be a part of any plan his club members might come up with. The look on his face last night when he was speaking was so determined; it made my heart swell in my chest in the strangest, scariest way. In that moment he looked like he meant every word, with a depth of passion I couldn't quite fathom. But if he means it, if he really won't allow me to be put in danger again, then maybe there's another way.

Rebel just shakes his head at me. "Don't get any ideas, Sophia. I know this shit is fucked up. I know I should have just let you go when Julio handed you over, but I was too angry to see straight then. I've been even angrier since we left my father's place." He laughs shakily, pressing a hand into his side. "Funny how losing an obscene amount of blood can make a guy cool his heels and start thinking properly again. I'm not normally the guy who runs into a situation guns blazing. I'm the guy who figures out how to disarm everyone without them even realizing." A shadow passes over his face, the light in his eyes dimming. "That tactic's not going to work out this time. This time there will be blood and people will die, and I don't want you anywhere near it. This can't last longer than a couple more days, okay? Once it's all over, I'll personally make sure you're delivered back to Seattle safe and sound without a hair on your head harmed. If that's what you want..."

"*If that's what I want?*" I almost can't breathe around the words. They just seem so ludicrous. "Why *wouldn't* it be what I wanted?"

Rebel just lies there, still covered in blood like something out of a horror show, looking at me. His inhales slowly, then lifts his hand and holds it out to me. "I'm done with the bullshit. If you want me, it won't be pretty. I know I sure as fuck don't deserve you, but I think you're a smart girl. You can feel what's right around the corner for us, right? You can sense how consuming and desperate and explosive it will be if we both just take one step forward. I'm not saying it's not ridiculously dangerous to be with me. To be the partner of someone who lives the kind of life I lead. But *you*...if there's anyone in this world with enough backbone and stubbornness to survive it, it's *you*. And you'd more than survive here, Sophia. You'd flourish."

There's a huge, painful lump in my throat by the time he's finished. My cheeks feel like they're on fire. Every encounter I've had with a guy before has been awkward and shy in the beginning. So much beating around the bush. Reading in between the lines. 'Dating,' where no one has a clue where they stand. With the man lying in front of me in this bed, there is no hidden meaning. He's afraid of nothing. He knows what he wants and he speaks plainly. It's terrifying.

"I—"

"You need to think about it. And that's okay. But know this. If you want to be with me, everything will change for you. No more college. No more middle class existence. I'll make you feel like you were sleeping before, like you have no idea how you lived such a placid, quiet existence without me." His voice deepens, sending thrills through me. "I'll fuck you raw, Soph. I'll make you forget what it was like to be with any other man. I'll ride you so hard, you won't remember your own name. I'll be the only thing tethering you to this earth. My sheets will be soaked with your come every single damn night for the rest of your sublime existence. This I promise you."

I feel like I'm seconds away from passing out. *Holy. Fucking. Shit.* No one... *no one* has ever spoken to me like that before in my entire life. And the crazy thing is that I know it's true. I know he means every single word, and more importantly he can deliver. I have absolutely no idea what I'm supposed to say in return to that. Rebel's still holding his hand out to me, waiting for me to do something.

He did the same thing in the hallway at his father's place, asking me to accept him, but I was saved from making any sort of decision by the blood-curdling scream that came from Louis James Aubertin II's kitchen at the time.

There's no one screaming now, though. I take a deep breath, trying to think of something appropriate to say while at the same time assessing what I even *want* anymore. I draw a total blank. "You realize that's impossible, right?" I whisper. "That a girl can't soak sheets with her come."

Rebel lowers his hand. His eyes shine, some sort of mischevious mirth hidden there, just behind the sharpness of his gaze. "You think the female ejaculation is a myth?"

"Isn't it?"

He starts laughing, deep in the back of his throat. It's a wicked, dangerous sound. "Oh, boy. Sounds to me like you've never come properly before, Soph. And that's a crying shame." The laughter dies on his lips, transforming his expression into one of deadly seriousness. "If you let me, I'll be *more* than happy to rectify the situation."

He fixes me with those ice-blue eyes of his, so disturbingly beautiful, and I feel like I'm about to squirm out of my own damn skin. I could barely look into them when we first met, and that hasn't really changed.

And now, with him talking about female ejaculation, I'm finding it hard to think straight. "You shouldn't be making bold threats like that, you jerk," I inform him. "You could *not* deliver on that."

He grins. "How little you know me."

Rebel sleeps some more. I find myself watching him, panic coursing through my veins. Three weeks. I can't believe I've only been gone for three weeks. I feel my throat tightening shut when I realize I've missed my mom's birthday. It just slipped me by without notice. Usually Sloane and I will take her out for a girls' day, usually coffee and breakfast in the morning, followed by a spa session, mani-pedis and massages all round. It's been our staple celebrating for the past five years.

The ridiculous thing is that neither my sister or my mother are the kinds of people to enjoy spa days. Sloane was always too focused on her studies and then on her internship, and my mom still thinks every last cent that comes into the house should be squirreled away, banked, invested or donated to the church.

Mom's birthdays are usually awkward affairs.

And this year, instead of getting my toenails trimmed like a prize Pomeranian, I was fucking Rebel in a hallway. Literally. My mom was probably crying hysterically from the moment she woke up to the moment she went to sleep.

"Hey. Hey, what's up?" Rebel reaches up slowly and trails blood-stained fingertips across the line of my jaw. His touch sends violent shivers chasing through my body. I don't even want to mention where the sensation settles, growing and growing with an increasing sense of urgency. I take his hand and place it back on his chest.

"I'm fine. Just still...y'know. *Dealing.*"

"Yeah. Dealing's pretty shitty." He looks down at himself—he's such a mess—and I want to laugh at how insufficient the statement is. I don't think my body remembers how to laugh anymore, though. Screaming or total, terror-filled silence seem to be the only two functions my vocal chords are capable of.

"Your guys all saw me last night," I say, trying to keep my eyes off Rebel's bare chest. I'm morbidly fascinated by the angry red stitches that trail across his stomach and disappear over his side, toward his back. His blood has dried and cracked, turned so dark it's almost black; it creates bizarre patterns all over the tightly packed muscle of his chest and stomach. "I say guys," I continue, "but there were two women there, too. An older, really tall woman, and a younger one with pink hair."

Rebel nods. "Yeah. Fee. Josephine. She's the tall one. She was one of the first club members. And the one with the pink hair..." He shakes his head ruefully. "That one is the bane of my fucking life. The rest of the crew are guys, though. Did any of them look like they were going to lynch you?" he asks.

"They looked stunned actually. Seems like you did a really good job of keeping me a secret."

Rebel purses his lips—god, I want to bite them. I can still remember how amazing they felt all over my body—and then he blinks up at the ceiling, like he's weighing up what he wants to tell me. Eventually, he says, "They're good guys. The Widow Makers isn't like any other club, though, Soph. Everyone has a story here. There isn't a single person here who joined because they think breaking the law is fun. We have a lot of vets here. Like me. Like Cade. After the corps chews you up and spits you out, you kinda feel like...like you've lost your family. Unless they're ex-military too, your blood and bone relatives will never understand what you've been through. The bond you build with the other guys in your unit...they're never *just guys* by the end. Even the guys you hate, the ones who drive you insane, the ones you wanna kill half the time—they're your brothers too." He laughs. "I mean, most brothers want to strangle each other half the time anyway, right? But if someone fucks with them..." Shaking his head, Rebel sighs. "Someone tries to fuck with them and it's game on. Brothers will defend each other 'til the death.

"And these guys who somehow found their way to me, they're even more gung-ho about that stuff than the army. Ramirez has been screwing with me and my family for years now, screwing with our business. These men aren't going to take that lying down. They're going to skin the motherfucker alive, given half the chance. They'll do it by any means necessary. They won't let a girl they don't know get in their way. And some of them haven't exactly had the most stable female role models in their lives, either. A few of them…a few of them don't see a reason for there to be women around the club at all, other than for the occasional receptacle to sink their dicks into.

"I didn't want them getting confused about your purpose here, Soph. So, yeah. You were pretty much the most heavily guarded secret I had. That's seriously saying something. And, no, I'm *not* sorry for it."

REBEL

The next five days are seriously fucking shitty.

Moving is a uphill struggle—even getting up to take a piss is a monumental effort—and when I do feel well enough to sit up in bed, I'm not even allowed to hold a goddamn book. Cade told Sophia not to let me lift anything and, boy, did the girl take him literally. She reads to me. She fucking *reads* to me, and it's amazing. I don't tell her that, though. I sit with my eyes closed, pretending I don't notice *her* eyes are on *me* more often than they are on the pages of Catch 22.

Unlike the first night I was hurt, she doesn't sleep with me in the bed anymore. She sleeps on the couch, arms and legs contorted in the most amusing positions, hair wild and crazy all over the cushions.

I can't believe she's never come properly. That in itself is a travesty. I mean, yes, she came with me in that hallway, but that was rushed, a spur of the moment thing. Definitely not my best work. I can make her come so much harder than that. I can make her feel like her whole body is being ripped apart at the seams if I want to. And I do. I want to open her eyes. I wanna be the guy to show her what sex can feel like if it's done properly, by a real man and not by some pissy, soft college kid. I'm gonna turn her whole world on it's head, and it is going to be so goddamn perfect.

In between what's going down with Ramirez, Dela Vega, and the gigantic fucking hole in my side, I'm sure thinking about a girl is the most insane thing I could be doing right now, but as I lie in bed, staring at the ceiling, Sophia is the only thing occupying my mind.

She may think she's being smart by sleeping on the other side of the room, but she's not as clever as she thinks she is. I've seen the way she looks at me. She's the most transparent person on the face of the planet—every thought she has is usually displayed right there on her face for everyone to see. It's actually quite dangerous, really. Tonight I witnessed her thinking very bad things about me at least three times before she said she was tired and decided to bundle herself up to sleep, and it took every last scrap of will power I possessed to not physically pin her to the mattress and fuck her stupid. If I weren't in so much pain, I would have done it, too.

I think about that instead of the exposed wooden beams over my bed. I think about getting her on all fours so I can lick her pussy from behind. That quickly progresses into me sliding my fingers inside her as I lick and suck. Despite the burning pain lighting up my side, my cock begins to harden as I get a little more adventurous. By the time I've got her sitting on my face, my dick is rock solid and demanding I do something about the throbbing ache. I can't believe I'm horny. I can't believe I'm even still awake, considering the two healthy doses of morphine Cade shot me up with earlier. I've always burned off drugs really fast, though. And my cock's never seemed to know when the hell it should be behaving itself.

I try to ignore the growing desire pulsing around my body. I try to sleep. Across the other side of the room, Sophia turns over, the oversized shirt hitching up to expose bare flesh across her stomach. And her panties.

Fuck.

For a Seattle girl, she's rocking a killer tan. And a killer body to match it.

Go to sleep, Jamie. I try to talk myself into shutting her out, into letting unconsciousness slip over me, but the more I let go of the grip I'm holding on my thoughts, the more they wander to the half naked woman on the other side of the room.

"Jesus," I whisper softly under my breath. "This is going to end badly." I last another minute before I've had enough. I need to act, need to do something about this. I have to.

Getting up is really not fun. I have to tense my abs to hold everything in tight, which naturally hurts when you've just had minor surgery. I feel like if I cough, my intestines are going to burst right out of me all over the floor.

Once I'm sitting upright, I carefully get to my feet. The room seesaws and I have to reach out to brace against the wall before I fall over. Yeah, this is a really bad idea indeed. I'm probably going to pass out well before I make it to Soph.

Still. Loss of consciousness in the pursuit of epic sex is definitely worth it.

With all the speed of a ninety-five year geriatric, I slowly, gradually make my way across the cabin. My head actually clears a little from the movement, which is good and bad in turns. Means I can feel even more, but I can piece my fractured ideas and thoughts together a little better too. Fair trade.

I stare down at Sophia, wondering what she's dreaming about. She's so beautiful. When I was a kid, my mother had a print of Gustav Klimt's 'The Kiss' on her bedroom wall. I used to stand and stare at the fine detailing of that painting, admiring the obvious, captured emotion between the two subjects, and admiring how ethereal the woman looked. That's how Sophia looks now—ethereal. Not of this world. Magical, somehow. She takes my breath away.

I should feel a little guiltier about what I'm about to do, but I don't. She's not going to object. She's going to enjoy every last second of it, even if it kills me. And if I'm wrong and she doesn't want it, I'll stop and she can kick my ass again. Slowly I sink down to my knees and carefully hook my fingers under the waistband of her black cotton panties. The backs of my hands make contact with her sides and her skin is scalding, hot to the touch. She stirs, moaning lightly. I freeze, but then kick myself. The goal isn't to *not* get caught here. I want her awake and writhing against me, damn it. I want her panting my name as I make her come.

I bite back a smile as I let go of her panties, changing tack, and slowly sliding my thumb down, in between her legs. She inhales sharply, back arching up a little from the sofa, but she remains asleep. Her body responds to me, even though she's out cold, which is a beautiful thing. She opens her legs, sliding them apart, sending blood rushing to my head.

She is so amazing. Her body is incredible. My dick presses persistently against my boxers, but I don't touch myself. This will be so, so much better if I wait for her to lay hands on me. I start slowly, rubbing her clit with my thumb in small circles. This is such delicious torture. I want to pull her underwear to the side and taste her, but it's too soon. I want her to be awake for that. I want her to *want* me to. I apply a little more pressure with my thumb, a slow smile spreading across my face as Sophia gradually presses her hips up, grinding herself against me. Mind blowing.

As I lightly press my mouth against the inside of her thigh, I look up the length of her stunning body to see that her eyelids are fluttering open. I guess this is the decisive moment. I ready myself, bracing for the full force of her outrage. Her lips part, the tip of her pink tongue slowly sliding out to wet her lips. She gazes at me blearily. I witness the moment where she fully comprehends what's happening as her eyes clear of sleep, growing wider.

"What—?"

I hold up my free hand, halting her before she can go any further. "Don't kick me. If you kick me, you'll open up my stitches."

"Will I open up your stitches if I kick you in the head?" she whispers.

I nod. "Probably. And let's face it. You might mess up my face. You like my face. You don't want to mess it up."

"You really are something else," she says. She doesn't bat my hand away, though. She doesn't tell me to stop. I press down a little hard, quickening the motion as I continue to tease her clit, and she holds her breath.

"I can stop if you want me to, Soph. I can drag my ass back to my bed, no problem. I get the feeling you don't want me to, though."

"You're an arrogant son of a bitch. What makes you think—"

"Because I can feel how wet you are through your panties, Sophia. And you're really, really damn wet."

"Urgh!" She presses her legs together, trapping my hand between them, scowling at me where I'm kneeling on the floor beside her.

"What now?" I ask, grinning at her. "Is this where you pretend to get all upset and make me remove my hand? Huh?" I have just enough room to continue stroking my fingers over her pussy. She tenses, the muscles in her legs locking up. I can see the need in her eyes, which is almost enough to make me forget rational thought. "*Or* is this when you open up for me and let me slide my index finger and my middle finger deep inside you while I use my mouth on you at the same time."

"You are *not* going down on me," she hisses.

"Why not?"

"Because. I haven't showered since this morning." Her scowl deepens, but I can see her true feelings quite plainly in her eyes again. The idea of my tongue lapping at her clit is turning her on. In case I needed any further evidence, I can feel her panties growing even wetter. They're soaked now. The need to taste her is almost overwhelming, but I manage to restrain myself. I have to wait for her to unclamp her legs from around my arm before I can do anything anyway.

"Sophia," I whisper. "There's no one else here. This is just you and me. Are you afraid of me?"

"I should be."

"Maybe. But *are* and *should be* are two different things. Are you attracted to me?"

She swallows. It looks like it takes great effort. "Yes," she says breathlessly.

"Good. And do you think I'm going to hurt you?"

Answering this question takes a little longer. She stares me dead in the eye, not blinking or breathing while she makes up her mind. Eventually she says, "No."

"Good. Do you think I'm going to try and make you do something you don't want to?"

She slowly shakes her head.

I quicken my movements, rubbing her a little more firmly. Her eyes practically roll back in her head. "Say it," I command. "Tell me you know I won't force you to do anything you don't want to."

"I know you won't force me," she says, sighing. "Oh god..." She closes her eyes altogether.

"Open your legs for me, sugar."

"No, I—" I begin to pull my hand away, ready to back the hell off, but she locks her legs together even tighter. "How about...a *trade*?" she asks.

"I'm not very good at compromising."

"So I've gathered."

"So what do you want to trade?"

"I'll open my legs...if you let me out of here. I want free roam of the compound. Whenever I want."

"No. Not happening." There's just no fucking way. I tug my hand back, trying to free myself, but she's got a pretty damn good hold on me.

"You said it yourself, Rebel. I'm safe here. What could be the harm?"

"You're even more safe in this cabin, sugar."

She gives me a look that I'm sure caused her daddy to melt like butter whenever she wanted something she knew she wasn't allowed. She has that look nailed, damn it. Regardless that I'm aware she's manipulating me, I find myself caving. If she were just in the compound when I knew it was safe, that would surely be okay. A month ago, there's no way I would even be considering this, but now...now she's had plenty of time to work her way under my skin, and I'm in some serious trouble. I really can*not* believe I'm about to agree to this. "All right. Fine. But only when I'm here. Or Cade." I don't know who's more surprised—me, or her. She blinks at me, owlish, and then smiles.

"Thank you."

"Show me how grateful you are. Open your legs for me, sugar."

She doesn't do it for a second, but then she gradually releases the tension in her legs, freeing my arm. In doing so, she's given my free rein to proceed at my own pace. Pulling her panties to one side, I carefully dip my fingers into the slick, wet heat of her pussy. Her face blossoms into an expression of horror when I raise my fingers to my mouth and suck on them.

"Shit no! Don't. Don't *do* that!"

I smirk mercilessly. "Why not?"

"I already told you! I haven't showered since this morning. I'm gross. I'm—I'm *dirty*."

"Oh, sweetheart, you are *not* dirty. You are fucking perfect. You pussy looks, smells and tastes incredible. I'm literally fighting with myself here. I wanna bury my face in there and make you come all over my tongue. It's driving me insane."

Sophia's face loses all color. "You just...can't, okay? It's too embarrassing."

I laugh. "I promise you, sugar, one day very soon you're gonna be begging me to light you up with my tongue. You're gonna crave it more than air. In the meantime, fine. I'll just use my fingers instead."

She looks like she wants to argue with that too, but I slide my fingers inside her before she can get another word out, and the look of sheer pleasure on her face has me fist pumping on the inside. She's so responsive. She reacts to my every tiny movement. She doesn't know it yet, but she's the perfect sexual partner for me. I love to know how the girl I'm fucking is feeling; making a woman moan is the most basic but greatest pleasure in my life. I wouldn't trade it for anything.

Sophia moans for me even as I'm thinking this. Her breath catches in her throat, telling me that I've hit the right spot.

I wonder what she'd do if I did try and make her come properly right now. She'd be freaked out, no doubt. It's not a normal sensation for a woman. She'll feel like she's about to pee everywhere and that will shut her down instantly. No. We'll have to wait on that one. If I get my way, which I definitely intend on doing, then there will be plenty of other times to adventure into unknown orgasm territory.

Sophia's muscles spasm as she tries to fight against the sensations rolling over her body. It's the most amazing thing, watching her wage this kind of war with herself. It's a war she won't win, because no matter how angry it makes her, and how badly it makes her feel like she's losing something somehow, she *wants* me. She wants my fingers inside her, and she wants my tongue working over her clit.

It's not long before my own wants start to make themselves known. I want to fuck her. I shouldn't even be thinking about that—I'm in no position to be undertaking that sort of physical exertion—but sometimes the human body can shock and amaze. Or rather, be annoyingly stubborn and persistent until it gets what it wants. I could make Sophia come now if I wanted to. It wouldn't take much. She's ready to tumble over the edge, and all it would take from me is a little extra pressure, and a little more speed. I hold off, though. She makes a stifled groaning sound when I stop altogether.

"You want something significantly bigger than my fingers inside you, sugar?" I ask, keeping my voice low. Her pussy tightens around my fingers, and I know the idea excites her.

"You're not...sticking anything weird inside me," she says, her voice hoarse.

I can't help it; I chuckle under my breath. "Now why would I want to do that when I have a perfectly good, perfectly hard cock ready and waiting?"

Sophia glances at me down the length of her body. Her hair is mussed and gathered about her face, and her lips are plump and swollen...so fucking sexy. She lifts one eyebrow, arching it for me. "You really do have a death wish, don't you?"

"If I *do* die, make sure Cade gets my bike."

"Why don't you just...not..." She can't finish her sentence, though, because I've started circling my fingers inside her again, and it apparently feels really good. She's gonna feel a million times better when I fuck her.

I can't hold off any longer. My blood is roaring in my ears as I stand up and take hold of her thighs, pulling her roughly down the couch toward me. I still haven't taken her panties off, but there's something really hot about having them pushed to the side, exposing her pussy, so I leave them on. Sophia watches with wide eyes as I push my boxers down over my hips, and then kick them off.

I take my cock in my hand, slowly pumping my fist up and down the hard muscle, shivering slightly at the pressure. It really isn't normal that I'm feeling this way, but if I don't get myself inside her so I can feel that perfect little pussy of hers tightening around me then my balls are going to explode. She probably doesn't even realize she's doing it, but Sophia's digging her fingernails into her thighs, causing the flesh under her nails to turn from blushed pink to white. She wants me. She wants me bad. She doesn't look at my cock, though. It's like she's afraid of it or something. Give her a few weeks and she'll be intimately acquainted with it. This coyness will be long gone. I'm willing to put money on it.

Sliding myself forward, she sucks in a sharp breath when the head of my dick is pressing against her pussy. She seems a little hesitant, so I use it to rub up and down over her clit, over the opening of her pussy. She locks up when I move back a little, toward her ass, so I change direction and focus on the areas she seems okay with. When she starts angling her hips up every time I slide myself over her pussy, I know she's ready.

I take no prisoners. I'm not rough enough to hurt her, to cause her any kind of pain whatsoever, but her eyelids snap open when I thrust myself inside her, all the way, balls deep. "Oh...*shit*," she hisses.

"You have such a dirty mouth." I fold myself over her, not paying any attention to the stabbing pain that sings through me, and take hold of her breasts through the t-shirt she's wearing. No bra underneath. Perfect. Her tits are soft and full, pliable under my hands. She may not do it willingly but her back curves away from the couch, lifting her chest, offering herself to me. I don't need telling twice. I grab the hem of the t-shirt and yank it upwards, revealing her incredible body. Her nipples are tight already, turned a dark pink, flushed with blood. She moans breathlessly when I take her right breast in my hand, palming it roughly. At the same time, I take her other nipple into my mouth and I carefully squeeze it between my teeth.

I've remained very still inside her, enjoying the intense reactions she has every time I shift ever so slightly, but now I start to move again, drawing myself all the way out of her before driving myself back in, slowly but firmly.

"Oh...*ohmygod.*" Avoiding my half healed side, she hooks her left leg around me, pulling me closer to her as I thrust, and the extra force is enough to drive me fucking crazy.

I can't stop now. Even if I did split my stitches, I would have to make her come before I could stop this. I need to feel her body seizing up tight. I need to hear the sound of her breath quickening. I need to watch her expression change as the tidal wave of pleasure slams into her.

I'm desperate for all of that to happen, but I'm also a major fucking tease, too. I bring her so close to climax, having to stave off coming myself at least three times before I can't take it anymore.

It sounds like her screams are being ripped out of her throat by force as I slam myself into her over and over again, rolling her clit with my thumb at the same time as I fuck her. I rarely come at the same time as a woman—I'm always far too intent on watching the whole thing play out—but this time I don't have a choice. She opens her eyes at the last second, dark chocolate irises locked right on me, and she whispers my name, my *real* name, and I'm screwed.

I come with her, our bodies both tense and gripped in ecstasy for what feels like minutes but can only really be seconds, and then we're melting together. I rest my forehead against her collarbone, panting, trying to clear my vision of the small starburst of color exploding like fireworks.

"So...is Cade going to be claiming ownership of your bike by morning?" Sophia says softly. She strokes her hand up and down over the skin of my back, oblivious to the fact that she's practically making my eyes roll back in my head.

"The fucker isn't getting that bike for a long time yet," I tell her. "Not until we get to do that at least three or four more times."

She laughs quietly, and it's a fucking remarkable sound.

SOPHIA

My body aches. Burns, in fact. I want to lie still, to sleep forever, or at least another few hours anyway, but I can't. An incessant pounding on the cabin door wakes me before dawn, though the loud hammering doesn't wake Rebel. Seems he can sleep though just about anything. Unsurprising, given how late he stayed up last night, how much morphine he had in his system and how energetic he'd been when he'd pinned me to the couch and fucked me. I'd had to spot him as he weaved his way back across the other side of the cabin, and then he'd pulled me into his bed, refusing to let me go back to sleep on my own. I feel hung over as I disentangle myself from his arms and get up, pulling my t-shirt down to cover my bare legs.

"Rebel? Rebel, man, open up!" a gruff voice hisses. I can tell by the sharp tone of the male voice on the other side of the door that it's Cade, and that he's also super pissed. "*Rebel, open the fucking door.*"

"All right, already," I hiss back. Despite the low light coming from a lamp on the other side of the room, I still manage to stub my toe as I hurry across the room to get the door. My foot is throbbing and my heart is beating out of my chest when I open up, glaring at the two dark figures lurking on the porch. Not just Cade, then—Carnie, too.

"Is he okay?" Cade asks briskly.

"Yeah. Yeah, I think so," I reply. "He's out cold." Carnie gives me a none too subtle once over, his eyes raking over my bare legs, and it's with a considerable horror that I realize I'm not even wearing any underwear. He can't see anything, but I still suddenly feel very naked. Cade gives Carnie a pointed look, clearing his throat, at which point the other man looks away, eyes to the sky.

"We need to come in," Cade tells me. "It's important."

"I gathered, since you were trying to knock the damn door down." I pluck at the t-shirt, trying to pull it down some more as I move aside to let them in. I close the door behind them and Cade beelines straight for the bed where Rebel is still passed out on his back, a very thin sheet barely covering his naked form. Cade clears his throat, scratching at his jaw. He seems to think about how to proceed before grabbing hold of his friend and shaking him hard enough to make his head bounce off the pillow.

Rebel is instantly awake, eyes wide, fist pulling back as he readies to punch Cade. "What the fuck?" he snaps.

"No time for pleasantries," Cade says. "Can you walk?"

Rebel inhales, pulling a deep breath into his lungs. He glances between the three of us, and then nods, resting his hand over his injured side. "I might be able to if you quit shaking the shit out of me, man. What's going on?"

"We got a problem," Carnie says softly. "A big one. You need to see."

Cade grunts. "You need help getting dressed?"

Rebel shakes his head. "Give me a beat. I'll be out in a second."

Cade and Carnie leave without saying another word, both of them wearing grim, frightening expressions on their faces. I've never seen either of them look so angry. Cade's always polite with me, well mostly, anyway, and yet it's like he doesn't even see me as he exits the cabin. I don't know why, but a sense of intense foreboding settles over me. Something really awful has happened. Something beyond compre-hension. Something I probably don't want to know about. A wave of panic sings through my veins—panic not for myself, but for Rebel. He's nowhere near fully recovered, and knowing his luck he's probably about to be shoved head-first into a really dangerous situation again.

Slowly, he heaves himself into a sitting position, pressing his hand into his side, wincing in pain. His beautiful body is in bad shape, black and blue, his bruises visible even against the complex, dark background of his extensive tattoos.

"Are you sure you should be moving about?" I ask. "Shouldn't you be resting for a couple more days at least before you head off on some wild goose chase in the early hours of the morning?"

"If Cade comes in here looking like he just did, it means something important requires my attention. He wouldn't ask me to come if it wasn't entirely necessary. So yeah, I have to go."

"Couldn't he just tell you what the hell has happened?"

"In case you haven't noticed, Sophia, Cade is not that wordy. He's more of a show than a tell guy." He winks, groaning as he carefully gets to his feet. I want to give him more morphine, but I get he still has a huge supply of the drug coursing through his circulatory system. More at this point could kill him. Dad used to tell me about that all the time—people who overdose on painkillers, both unintentionally and intentionally, and slip away without even so much as a by-your-leave. It happens so easily. They're dangerous things, painkillers. And highly addictive to boot.

"You feel like passing me a pair of jeans?" Rebel jerks his head toward his closet, brow furrowed in pain. "I think you'll get there quicker than me."

I open up the door to his closet to find the most immaculately organized walk-in I've ever seen. T-shirts, shirts, belts, shoes—everything is placed and folded just so. Puts my room back on campus to shame. I like to think of my room as organized chaos, but the truth is it's actually just chaos. I grab a pair of jeans, boxers and a t-shirt for him, and then I watch as he fights his way into his clothes. I'm about to ask him if he needs me to help him at one point but he holds his hand up as soon as I take a step toward him. The look he shoots me could freeze over hell. Eventually, after a good ten minutes of swearing under his breath, he's fully dressed. I can tell the effort has cost him a lot, though. His face is pale, his forehead lightly speckled with sweat, and he doesn't seem that steady on his feet.

"Are you coming?" Cade calls through the closed door.

"Jesus wept, man! I have a fucking hole in my side," Rebel yells back. He starts to cross the room and I quickly snatch up my own jeans, kicking them on in record time.

Rebel gives me a curious look, arching an eyebrow at me. "Where do you think you're going?"

"With you."

"No, you're staying here."

"Funny, because I was sure you told me a couple of hours ago I could have free roam of the place if I wanted. Did I imagine that?" It takes me a second to realize my hands are on my hips, my own eyebrows raised in challenge. He'd better not take that back. He promised me I wouldn't be cooped up in here any longer. If he reneges on our deal, it won't matter what awful problem Cade and Carnie want to show him right now. He'll have a much bigger problem on his hands: *me*.

Rebel narrows his eyes. "I'm not saying you should stay here for the fun of it, Soph. It's for your own good."

"I'm an adult. How about you let me make my own decisions for once, huh?"

He stares at me a second longer before rolling his eyes. "Okay, fine. But remember, whatever happens, this was your call."

I drop my hands from my hips, trying to hide my surprise. "Great. Thank you."

Outside, Cade takes one look at me and shakes his head. "You won't want her seeing this, man."

Rebel casts a look at me over his shoulder, a guarded look in his pale blue eyes. "She's an adult, Cade. She can make her own decisions, apparently."

A hundred meters from the compound gate, a lone tree stands by the side of the dirt road, silhouetted against the rising sun. From the moment we leave the gate, making slow progress as Rebel hobbles after Cade and Carnie, I can see that something's not right. It's not until we're much, *much* closer that I catch sight of the reason why Cade seems to be so agitated though.

A body.

A body hangs from the tree, upside down, suspended by one foot. The other leg hangs at an awkward angle. The foot which should be at the end of that leg is missing. The hands which should be at the ends of the arms hanging freely below are also missing. And the head... the head is gone, too. Blood mottles the naked flesh, covering the torso, the buttocks, the legs...

The rope, looped around the thick bough of the tree, creaks as the body spins, facing us, revealing that it's the body of a woman. There's what looks like a scrap of blood stained paper stuck to her body, black writing typed across it, but I don't see what it says. I drop to my knees instead, and vomit into the red dirt beneath me.

"Jesus. *A gift, from Los Oscuros?* What the fuck is wrong with this guy?" Rebel hisses. From where I'm bent over double on the ground, I can see that his hands are shaking. I lock onto that sight, willing myself not to look up at the poor woman hanging from the tree, at the awful things that have happened to her. Rebel's hands shake and shake and shake. And the woman's hands are...are just *gone*.

Cade grunts. "And what the fuck is up with their choice of font, too?"

"Yeah." Carnie spits on the ground. "Really says a lot about your intentions. I mean, how are you meant to take someone seriously when the message they send you is printed in motherfucking comic sans?"

"You cut their body into small pieces. That's how you take them seriously. Hector's fucking with us," Rebel says softly. They continue to talk, but my ears are ringing. I can't focus on the subdued conversation that takes place over me, but I can feel the tension pouring off the three men. I can literally taste their rage. I throw up again, screwing my eyes shut, unable to breathe.

Oh my god. I can't... I can't... I can't...

"Bron," Cade says. "Her name's Bron. She's Keeler's girl. I recognize the tattoo." I make the mistake of looking up, then. I see the small tattoo of a rose on the inside of her right forearm, just above her wrist. The bloody stump where her arm terminates is still dripping blood. I heave again, though nothing comes up this time.

"Fuck." Rebel sinks to his knees beside me, his face now completely ashen, devoid of all color. He reaches for me, pulling me to him, though he doesn't really look at me. He's staring at the piece of mutilated flesh hanging from the tree like a slaughtered cow. Slowly, he strokes a hand absently over my hair, the cool blue of his eyes hardening, darkening somehow, turning steely and cold. "Sick motherfucker," he whispers. "That sick, evil motherfucker picked her off because she wasn't inside the compound."

Cade laces his fingers behind the back of his head, turning away from the woman. He squints into the distance, out into the desert, his mouth pulling down at both sides in a grimace. "Yeah. Yeah, looks that way."

"Does Keeler know?"

Carnie kicks at the dirt, shaking his head. "No. No one else knows. I found her this morning when I came back from town. I went straight to Cade."

"Good. You did the right thing. I—*fuck*. God knows how we're gonna break this to everyone." Rebel sounds composed but his voice is utterly empty. I cry in his arms while he strokes my hair, wishing I hadn't been so damned stubborn. If I'd just let him have his way, I wouldn't have the image of Keeler's dead girlfriend burned into my memory. This isn't something that will ever go away. This isn't something I'll ever forget about. This is something that will give me nightmares for the rest of my life.

"They're gonna want blood," Cade says.

Rebel's chin rests on the crown of my head, and for some reason the intimacy of the action calms me a little. "I know," he says. "And they'll get it. We just have to make sure we go about this the right way. He's trying to bait us. Trying to provoke us. If we're angry when we go after him, we won't be thinking straight. We get sloppy, we make mistakes. This *has* to be contained."

"I hear you. But this woman had a foot, both her hands and her fucking head chopped off, Rebel. I'd like to see how you're gonna contain *that*."

REBEL

Turns out Keeler spent the night away from the compound, visiting his sister in Cedar Crest. At the moment he's one of our primary tattoo artists at Dead Man's Ink, though. Today is his day to cover the shop, so Cade and I ride into town and to wait for him. We cut Bron's body down and drive her back to the compound first, of course, hiding her out of sight, where the other guys won't find her before we have chance to tell Keeler. Cade and I sit in the shop in silence, me bleeding through my stitches, staring at the walls, neither of us knowing what to say to one another. This isn't the first time we've seen fucked up shit. Afghanistan was a savage place. The things we saw there… That was the first time I really understood, really *knew* the evil man was capable of committing against his fellow man. Nothing will ever be more brutal than the atrocities we saw there. But this is different. This is here, on our fucking doorstep, and this isn't fucking Kabul. This is regular small town Americana, and this was one of our own.

Keeler's first appointment is at ten thirty, so Cade and I sit and stew for a good hour and a half before the low rumble of Keeler's motorcycle rattles the glass in the shop's window frames.

"How you gonna handle this?" Cade asks.

"I don't know. I guess we're about to find out."

Keeler looks surprised when he opens the shop door and finds Cade and me sitting at the counter. Concern flashes across his face. He's young, mid-twenties. Good guy. Not ex-army like most of the Widow Makers. He was beaten by his father from the moment he could walk til the moment he ran away from home—spent some time pin-balling between different drug gangs before he wound up on the wrong side of the law and serving three years for possession with intent to supply. He got his shit dialled in prison. He'd been out for a month when he walked through the doors of Dead Man's Ink for the first time, looking for work. Cade gave him a job on the spot. Took him a clean year to convince me to let him prospect for the club, though. Now I'm feeling really fucking guilty that I caved and swore him in.

"Hey, guys. What's up? Did I leave the door open or something?" He eyes us cautiously, like we're about to ream him out.

"No, dude. Come in. We gotta talk to you about something." I pull out a chair by the counter, gesturing for him to sit down. He looks like he's about to shit his pants.

"Uhhh... should I be freaking out right now? 'Cause I'm freaking out." He slowly walks into the shop and lowers himself into the seat.

"You haven't done anything wrong," Cade tells him. "It's—it's about Bron."

I watch the nervous smile fall from Keeler's face. "What about her?" he says slowly.

I take over. I'm the president of this club. I'm responsible for the people who have joined, and I should also be responsible for their loved ones. I should have known this was going to happen. I tell Keeler what's happened, doing my best to provide as few details as possible. It's impossible to keep the truth from him for long, though. The guy stares at me, as though I'm making it all up.

"Come on, man, stop fucking around. That shit ain't funny."

"I'm sorry. I swear to god, I am so sorry, and we are going to make this right, Key."

"She's dead? She's *dead*?"

"Yes."

"They...they cut off her *head*?"

I scrub my hands over my face, blowing all the air out of my lungs. "I'm sorry. Yes."

"Where is it?"

"What?"

"*Where is her fucking head, man?*" Keeler's voice is nothing more than a whisper, yet his eyes are screaming with rage. He's about to flip his shit.

"We don't know. We'll find out, though. We'll make this right." God, I really hope I'm not lying to this kid.

As predicted, Keeler explodes. Cade and I sit back and watch as he trashes the shop, punching a fist through the door to the back room, throwing the sterilizing equipment, destroying anything and everything he can get his hands on. We let him rage.

By the time he collapses into a heap on the floor, sobbing silently, shoulders jerking up and down as he weeps, there's barely a stick of furniture in the place that remains unbroken.

"Take him back to the compound," I tell Cade. Keep him away from everyone until I get back. No one leaves today, though. Tell the rest of the club they're on lockdown. Tell anyone with friends or family living here in town to make sure they pull everyone in. I'm not having his happen again."

Cade says he'll get it done and then leaves. As soon as he's managed to half carry, half drag Keeler out of the shop, I double over and clutch my side, breathing through the white hot, burning pain that's tearing through me. "Fuck." Breathing is hard again. I don't know if that's from the pain or from Keeler's complete devastation. He deserved better. He deserved for his girlfriend to be safe while he was out of town. I should have fucking known this was going to happen. Hector Ramirez is a sociopath. He's clinically insane. The life of an innocent bystander means nothing to him. He'd murder the entire town if he thought it would make his point. So I should have known.

"Well, that was quite the display."

My head snaps up at the sound of the voice, already knowing who it is. Already assessing how I'm going to proceed. Hector Ramirez stands in the open doorway of the shop, one hand braced against the frame, the other hand casually in the pocket of his suit pants. He looks mildly amused, like the scene of destruction before him is entertaining. His gaze settles on my side, my hand still pressing against my wound, and his eyebrows slowly rise. Taking *his* hand out of his pants, he places something small into his mouth and bites down on it, crunching.

"You know," he says. "It really is a shame you snuck up on my guards the other night. They're very jumpy men. They tend to react without thinking sometimes. If you'd simply have made your presence known to them and told them you wished to see me, I'm sure they would have treated you in a far more...*civilized* manner."

I grind my teeth together, mentally scanning the shop for a concealed weapon, something to do some serious damage to the evil piece of shit that is strolling into my property like he owns the damn place. Problem is, we don't keep guns or knives here. The shop's raided by the cops on a fairly frequent basis, and precautions have been necessary in the past.

With a slight grunt of distaste, Hector steps over the smashed coffee table between he and I, his leather shoes crunching as he treads on shards of glass. "I imagine you found my little gift this morning?" he says. "I worried that you might not see her. Raphi suggested we leave our present to you right on your doorstep where you wouldn't miss it, however that seemed a little too obvious. I didn't want the police arresting you for murder because there was a mutilated corpse propped up against your boundary wall. Where would the fun have been in that?" He puts something into his mouth again and chews—candied almonds. The bastard always has a pocket full of them. Makes him smell like an old woman.

I curl my fingers to make a fist, hate charging through my veins, seeping into my pores, infecting every last part of me with a rage that won't go unanswered. *Can't* go unanswered. I tried to do this the legal way, I really did. I wanted Ramirez and his men in jail for what they did to my uncle. I wanted them to suffer every horrifying, dark, awful violation possible while they served their time, knowing they were going to die as incarcerated men, never to walk free again. The time for that has past now, though. Now, I just want them all dead. Preferably in the most painful manner possible.

"You shouldn't have killed Leah. You should never have stepped foot on my father's property in Alabama. You should never have followed us back here, and you really shouldn't have harmed a hair on Bron's head, Hector. You think there won't be consequences?"

Hector Ramirez shrugs, pulling a fat cigar from the breast pocket of his suit jacket, apparently done with his almonds. He bites the end off the cigar and spits it onto the ground, then proceeds to light it with an engraved silver lighter. "From where I'm standing, the Widow Makers aren't the formidable force I assumed them to be when I undertook this little adventure to New Mexico, *Jamie*. When Raphi dealt with your uncle back in Seattle and your second in command made grand gestures, inciting war between our people, I thought to myself, '*well, okay now. This might be interesting. Something to distract you from the tedium of every day life, Hector. Thank the lord.*' But no. I arrive here to this dust bowl you call home, and I find a rag-tag group of misfits living out in the desert, sticking their dicks into the locals, *tattooing people for money.*" He gestures at the trashed shop, disgust warping his features. "I have to admit, I'm more than a little disappointed."

He makes it to the counter where I'm still bent double, trying to remain calm. Trying not to give away the fact that my right hand is resting on the one weapon we *do* keep in the shop—a prime maple Louisville slugger. I'm in a shit load of pain and my head is spinning, so I have to wait for the perfect moment. If I launch myself at him too early, I'm going down hard and I won't be getting back up again. That means I need him close. Closer than he is now, anyway. And that means I have to keep him talking.

"You made a huge mistake in coming here, Hector."

"Ahh, you think so?" He pouts, pulling on his cigar, holding the smoke in his mouth before he blows it out in a thick cloud. The smell reminds me of my father—he always smokes after dinner, ever the traditional southern gentleman. It takes me a mere second to connect the dots when I see the familiar Havana Red paper seal of my father's favorite brand wrapped around the rolled tobacco leaves in Hector's hand. He is *literally* smoking one of my father's cigars. This is an action designed to piss me off, to drive me crazy, but all he's succeeding in doing is distilling my anger into clarity. I don't see red. I don't react. My recklessness the other night, the recklessness that got me stabbed, isn't normally how I operate. Push me to the edge and I get smart. Poke and prod at my buttons and I come up with new and interesting ways to return the fucking favor. I've got my shit handled now, but then Hector Ramirez doesn't know that about me. He knows nothing about me whatsoever. He's massively underestimated both me and my club if he thinks he's going to succeed in baiting me into stupidity twice.

He comes closer, standing on the other side of the counter. "You know...I believe I recognized the woman with you at your father's home, Jamie. Can it be that you arranged for Julio Perez to purchase my little One Eighty-One on your behalf?"

One Eighty-One, the number he assigned to Sophia in order to sell her. Motherfucker. I glare at him, willing him dead. It's the only way I can maintain my relative calm. If he says her name...if he so much as mentions her again...

"That was very underhanded, you know. I can't say that I like you tricking me out of her like that. Bad business. My good friend Raphael has aired his concerns about her association with the Widow Makers. He's...*worried* about her safety. Normally, I'm careful to ignore Raphi's council, however in this particular instance I think he may have a point. *I want her back, Jamie.*"

My vision blurs in my peripherals, my heart rate doubling. No way. No fucking way is he having her. "You're certifiable if you think I'm handing her over to you, asshole."

Hector shakes his head, as though he expected more from me. He looks away, out of the shop window, biting down on the fat cigar in his mouth. "I'm sorry to hear that. But I suppose these things can't be helped. If you are not willing to return the girl to me, I will simply take her from you. You won't be able to stop me. And this way, when she is back within the confines of my household, performing for my pleasure, I will not treat her well, my friend. I will treat her like the whore she is. I will ruin her. I will make her obey me in everything. She will be degraded and tortured, and when I have had my fill of her, I will kill her. And this time I will make sure to send you her head and her hands instead of the rest of her body. No. I will keep the rest of her body. A pussy is still a pussy, after all, no?"

I don't feel the pain in my side anymore. My head is no longer fuzzy, my vision no longer blurred. Everything is crystal fucking clear, and my body is vibrating with fury. Only a second ago, I was clinging to the fact that his provocations wouldn't work on me, and I honestly believed that to be true. But now, with this? I *cannot* stay calm. I *cannot* keep a cool head. Sophia is a game changer. I swore I would protect her, and now Ramirez is threatening to violate her dead body?

No.

Just. Fucking. No.

He doesn't see the baseball bat coming. I whip it out from under the counter so fast that he has zero time to react before I'm swinging. Back in Alabama when I was a teenager, my father used to force me to stun his livestock with a sledgehammer before their throats were slit—'*one fierce blow to the temple, boy. What's the matter? Are you a fucking pussy or an Aubertin? God, you disgust me.*'

There were other, far more humane ways to end the animals' lives, but my father derived some kind of sick pleasure in watching me cry as I swung that sledgehammer at his cattle. He had me do it over and over again, hundreds of times. I hated every second of it, disorienting those cows so they could be slaughtered, but the experience taught me a lot. I've had plenty of experience. So when I slam the baseball bat into the side of Ramirez's head, it's with a precise and brutal force.

Ramirez's head rips around, the cigar flying out of his mouth. He drops down to one knee, making a low, gurgling sound at the back of his throat. Blood. There's blood all over the baseball bat, and Ramirez's head is pouring more of the bright red liquid down his face, soaking the crisp white collar of his shirt. I vault over the counter, already lifting the bat in my hands, ready to bring it down on his head again. I'm prepared to keep on lifting it and bringing it down until the man in front of me never gets up again. I can't have him hurting Sophia. I won't fucking allow it.

I'm two seconds away from landing another, terrible blow when Ramirez starts laughing. That was the gurgling sound he was making—laughter, while choking on the blood gathering in the back of his throat. "You...you really caught me with that one," he says, grinning. His teeth are covered in blood—bright white obscured by crimson. "Oooh, Jamie. You should see yourself," he growls, looking up at me, dark eyes burrowing into me. "You look fearsome. You look like the kind of man who's unafraid to kill another to protect what is his. Perhaps you're not such an unworthy adversary, after all. Your father was wrong. You do have a backbone."

"My father can go fuck himself. And so can you, motherfucker." I swing, and this time the bat connects with Ramirez's shoulder, sending him crashing to the floor. The crazy bastard curls up on his side amongst the shattered glass and laughs long and hard. He's insane. Has to be. He must know he's about to die, and yet his only response is this complete and utter hysteria. "Like I said," I growl. "You should never have come here, Hector." I raise the bat over my head, gripping it in both hands, and I'm ready. It's been a long, long time since I've killed a man, but this right now is well deserved. Hector killed Ryan. He killed Leah, and Bron. And now he's a threat to Sophia? I won't even feel bad about ending him. My conscience will be clear. There's nothing on earth that can stop me from finishing this, here and now.

It's at this exact moment that I'm thrown off my feet. It feels like I've been hit by a Mack truck. My back smashes against the counter, and my body wants to sink to the floor but I can't because my muscles have locked and my jaw is clenched so tightly that my teeth feel like they're going to shatter. Pain claims every nerve ending I own from my head to my toes. I can't make a sound, but if I could I'd be yelling out in agony.

Barely able to even move my eyeballs, I look down at the source of my pain and realize that there actually *is* something on this earth that could stop me. Two things, actually. The first, a fifty thousand volt Taser gun, the prongs of which are embedded into my chest. The second, the female police officer standing in the shop doorway.

"You wanna run that by me one more time, asshole?"

Detective Lowell, DEA, does not seem entertained by my response to her questioning. In fact, she looks severely pissed off. She likes things tidy. I can tell that just from looking at her—her immaculate gray pant suit, and her immaculately styled hair, and her immaculately understated make-up speak volumes. And questioning me in my messy, smashed up shop while two paramedics make sure I don't have any lasting injuries from where she shot me with her Taser is making her less than congenial. Funny, really, since I'm feeling so bright and shiny. If bright and shiny could also be described as fucking broken and in serious amounts of pain.

"I told you. I was just showing a prospective client some of our sporting memorabilia."

"I assume you're talking about the baseball bat?"

"Yes, ma'am."

"And you were showing it to him? By pile driving it repeatedly into his face?"

I glance up at her, wincing as one of the EMTs uses an alcohol swab to clean a cut above my right eye. "You saw me hitting that guy with my bat?" My tone of voice is borderline shocked. "That doesn't sound like something I would do at all."

Lowell exhales sharply, hands on her hips. "You had the thing held high over your head. Your *potential client* was prone on the ground, laughing. It sure as hell looked like you were about to use the thing to shut him up."

"Why would he have been laughing if I was beating him, Detective? That sounds crazy."

Lowell looks like she's about ready to pick up the bat and smash *me* over the head with it. She jerks her head toward the offending article lying on the ground where I dropped it. "Doesn't look like sporting memorabilia to me. Looks brand new."

"Not true. It's signed. Super valuable."

"I can't see a signature anywhere on that thing."

"It's there. It's just hidden underneath all the blood. See...*there*." I point. "David Ortiz."

David Ortiz hasn't signed the bat. But *I* did when we hid it under the counter. It's a fairly decent forgery. Lowell gives me a cold, dead-inside kind of look. "You think you're funny? You think this is a joke? This is jail time right here, buddy. Serious jail time."

"Detective, please. He's telling the truth." On the other side of the room, Ramirez is being aided by another EMT; his left eye has almost swollen shut and his arm is in a sling from where I dislocated his shoulder. "He was just showing me the bat," he says. "I fell and hit my head. I assure you, there was nothing untoward taking place when you shot at Mr Aubertin."

Lowell glances between the two of us, her brows drawn together, scowling furiously. "You're both horrendous liars. You think I don't know who you *both* are? You think I'm stupid? You think it's a coincidence that *I* am here, in the middle of bum-fuck-nowhere Hicksville, New Mexico, sitting here with the both of you? Because rest assured, it is *not*."

I shrug, giving her my best *I-don't-know-what-to-tell-you* face. "I'm no one special, Detective. I run a tattoo shop. And this gentleman—" I choke on the word. "—Just came in asking about getting some work done."

Lowell laughs a hard, stony laugh. "All right, just stop. Don't fucking bother. I'm sure I'll get the truth out of you back at the station. You're both under arrest." She reads me my Miranda rights first, and then repeats the process with Ramirez. As soon as the EMTs are done assessing me, I'm cuffed and bodily dragged out of the shop by two deputies. Ramirez isn't far behind. As I'm shoved into the back of a police cruiser, I catch Ramirez grinning at me out of the corner of my eye.

I know him. I know he won't change his story at the station, and neither will I. Lowell is about to be frustrated at every turn and I suspect I'm likely to spend the next twenty four hours in a holding cell, but I couldn't care fucking less. It'll give me time to think this thing through. It'll give me time to make plans.

I'm sure Hector Ramirez will do the same.

SOPHIA

I can't get the image of that headless woman out of my mind. It's there, every time I close my eyes for the rest of the day. Horrifying. The most awful thing I've ever seen. Rebel, Cade and Carnie kept their cool, but I could tell the sight had disturbed them, too. Rebel's hands were shaking as he walked with me back to the compound. Still shaking when he pulled me to him and lay with me on his bed for half an hour in silence as I cried.

He left me shortly after to go find the woman's boyfriend in town, and I've sat in his cabin ever since, staring at a wall, wondering how this can really be my life. I find myself thinking about Matt again. I made a choice to stay with Rebel back in Alabama. I've thought myself crazy many times since then. I could have gone back to my old life and to safe, boring Matt. I'd never have been exposed to mangled, headless corpses if I'd stayed with him. I'd have had a Costco account and checked out books from public libraries. I'd have visited wineries on the weekends and eventually had some kids and rescued a dog from the pound. I would have had a mundane, safe life I'm sure. Everything would have been fine.

But *Rebel*.

It's inexplicable. It's the worst decision I've ever made, and yet all the same, headless corpses or no, here I am, still sticking to it. What does that say about my mental state? It's dark by the time Rebel returns. He never told me what time to expect him back, so I haven't been worried, though when I catch sight of him that changes. He looks way, *way* worse than before if that's possible. He looks like he's literally nearly dead on his feet. Cade helps him through the cabin door and dumps him on the end of the bed, and I can do nothing but stare at him with my mouth hanging open.

"What...what the hell happened?" Rebel lies back on the bed, exposing the lower half of his stomach, which is red with fresh blood. It's then that I notice the two small holes in his black t-shirt. "And what the hell happened to your clothes?"

"He got hit with a Taser," Cade says dryly. "And then arrested by the DEA. I don't know, man. I leave you alone for five fucking minutes and look at the state of you."

Rebel groans. "I appreciate your concern."

"*What?*" My ears must be playing tricks on me. Rebel is so damned nonchalant, like being arrested and Tased is an every day occurrence. As soon as the thought hits me, I realize that perhaps it really *isn't* so uncommon for him, though. "You feel like explaining what happened?" I say.

"Love to. I kind of need a second, though," Rebel replies, pressing his knuckles into his sternum—he's in a lot of pain, though I know him well enough to know that he'll never say so.

"You should get into bed, man," Cade tells him.

"Not yet. We need to go to the clubhouse. The others will be raging if we don't explain all the cloak and dagger bullshit before the end of the day. They deserve to know."

Cade shakes his head, throwing his hands in the air. "Why the fuck did I just drag your ass up the damn hill, then?"

Rebel slowly turns his head to look at me. "Because we had to come get Sophia. It's time the rest of the club met her properly. I'm sure they're all asking questions."

Cade laughs. "That's one way of putting it. They were about ready to lay siege to this place this morning in order to find out who the hell she was."

Rebel's face takes on serious expression. "I hope you informed them how unwise that would be?"

"I did. And they didn't like it."

"They don't have to like it. They just have to do as they're told."

I haven't seen this version of Rebel before. He's angry, that much is obvious, but he seems focused, too. Determined. He's been intimidating since the first moment I met him, but right now he's downright scary. He looks at me again, taking a deep breath. "This is what you wanted, right? Free rein of the place. Freedom to see and talk to whomever you like? Well, this is it. Do you want to come with us to the clubhouse?"

I bite my lip, images of Costco and the fiction section of a Seattle public library flashing before my eyes. I slowly shake my head, feeling slightly hysterical. It's the challenge in his eyes. The look he gives me that tells me I need to be strong in order to immerse myself in this life.

I fold my arms across my chest, tilting my chin up in acceptance of his challenge. "Sure. Okay. I'll come."

Rebel's eyes flash cold steel. "Fuckin' A."

My memories of the clubhouse the other night are pretty hazy. I was too concerned with getting Cade to follow me back to Rebel in order to assess my surroundings, but now things are different. Now I have plenty of opportunity.

The place is cavernous—an old remodelled barn with high rafters and recast concrete floor. Long wooden tables and benches line the room, and smaller tables dot the edge of the space. A bar runs the length of the back wall, stocked with a multitude of different bottles of scotch as well as everything else you might expect to see in any normal bar.

There is a sea of people gathered inside, seated at the benches and hovering by the bar. Most are men, huge guys with arms full of tattoos, larger than life, scary as all hell. There are a few women and kids, too, all of whom look generally terrified and out of place. Everyone stops talking when they catch sight of Rebel. And me.

A woman at the back of the hall gets to her feet straight away. I recognize her—she was the woman who gave me the dirty look as I raced out of here behind Cade. She's different to the other women packed into the clubhouse. She's inked up, her nose pierced, pink hair pinned back in a messy topknot. She's wearing a torn Sepultura t-shirt and a snarl on her face that already spells trouble. Beside me, Rebel hangs his head, apparently sensing the same thing.

"What the fuck is going on, man?" she snaps. "We've been sitting here with our thumbs up our asses all day. Keeler's missing, and Cade hasn't told us shit. And who the fuck is *she*?" The woman stabs her finger at me like I'm an invading alien and she's ready to go Independence Day on my ass.

"Sit down, Shay. And shut your damn mouth. This isn't how we're doing things," Rebel says. His voice is monotone, controlled, but even I can tell he's irritated by her outburst.

The woman—Shay—shakes her head. "That's bullshit, Rebel, and you know it. You can't keep us in the dark, and you can't bring random women—"

"I SAID SIT THE FUCK DOWN AND SHUT YOUR GODDAMN MOUTH, SHAY!"

I nearly jump out of my skin as Rebel explodes. His face, completely colorless for the past five days, is suddenly bright red. His body is shaking, shoulders tensed, hands clenched into fists. "Today has been a seriously shitty day. Do *not* make it worse," he hisses.

Shay blanches, the hostility falling away from her. She looks very much like a frightened little girl, which I'm betting is a rare event. I'm also betting it's not very often that Rebel loses his cool; nearly every single person in the clubhouse looks stunned. Shay slowly sits down, and everyone else keeps their lips tightly sealed, clearly waiting for Rebel to speak.

Eventually he does. "This morning, Hector Ramirez sent us a very clear message. Carnie discovered the body of a woman hanging from a tree on the dirt road into town. It was Bron, Keeler's girlfriend. She'd been decapitated, her hands and one of her feet removed. Her body had been hung upside down from the tree."

The room explodes into sound. Forty people start shouting at once, the sound of their anger deafening. The obvious club members, the men with Widow Maker tattoos and leather cuts, are the angriest. In the corner of the room, a tall, skinny guy with long blond hair jumps out of his seat and rushes forward, limping ever so slightly. "Where the fuck is Keeler? And where the fuck is Ramirez? We have to kill the bastard. He's gotta fucking pay, Rebel."

Rebel blows out a deep breath. "Keeler's just taking a beat, Brassic. And Ramirez is holed up in a farmhouse on the other side of town. He was arrested this afternoon, as was I."

He goes on to explain that Ramirez showed up at their tattoo shop after Cade left and made some poorly veiled threats, at which point he'd laid into him with a baseball bat. I stand beside him, listening in horror as he goes through the motions of describing how he was then shot with a Taser and taken down to the local sheriff's department. Cue one very angry DEA agent, ten hours of very aggressive questioning, and then he was allowed to call Cade who came and got him. The tension in the room is at boiling point by the time Rebel finishes his story.

Brassic, the tall, blond guy who asked about Keeler, slams his palm down onto the table in front of him, sending an empty glass shattering on the floor. "When are we going after him, Rebel? We can't let this stand."

"And we won't. I know you're all angry. I'm angry, too. But we need to be smart. If you can come up with a solid plan of attack that doesn't end up in most of us dying and the rest of us in prison, I'd love to hear it. If not, then we need to take some time to figure this thing out. That DEA agent was intent on getting answers out of me. I'm sure she was the same with Ramirez. She told me plainly that she was in town with a crew, and that they weren't leaving until they get what they came for. That includes Hector Ramirez on charges for drug trafficking and murder, and the Widow Makers locked up for the LA shooting at Trader Joe's."

"We were cleared of that, man! The cops arrested the guys the Desolladors hired to frame us. They admitted everything!"

"I know that. You know that. Lowell knows that. She's pissed, though. Anything she can pin on us is a win for her. We're living under a microscope right now, guys. If we put one foot wrong, we're all fucked."

Rebel's words don't seem to have any effect. Or certainly not the one he's clearly hoping for, anyway. From the snatched words I overhear from people's conversations, it sounds like no one cares if they get caught, sent to prison, shot or killed. They just want revenge.

"You still haven't told us who *she* is," Shay repeats. She moderates her tone this time, but it's clear she's furious over my presence. Rebel fixes her in an artic stare.

"She was witness to my uncle's murder in Seattle. Hector and Dela Vega kidnapped her and we had Julio arrange purchase of her. She's my guest here, Shay. That's all you need to know."

"So Hector and Raphael found out you had her and came here looking for her, right?" A rumble of dissent goes up amongst the crowd. Shay can hardly keep the hatred from her face as she locks eyes on me. Rebel does something that surprises me next. He steps in front of me, blocking me from her view. "You look at her again like that, Shay, and you and me are gonna have problems. In fact, best not to look at her at all, you read me?"

"She's put us all in danger, Rebel. And you brought her here without telling any of us," she spits. "Don't you think we had a right to know about this? Don't you think it would have been smart to tell us if you were bringing danger to our doorsteps?"

"It sounds very much like you're questioning my judgement." Rebel's voice is all gravel and hard edges. He sounds like he's about to go off at the deep end. Cade places a hand on his shoulder but Rebel shakes it off.

He looks around the room—I can't see the expression on his face, but I'm betting it's terrifying. "This is not a democracy," he says slowly. "This is not a fucking day spa. You don't get to question me or go against my wishes. I've always done my best by you guys. I've always done my best to keep you safe. As of this moment, if any of you are unhappy with my leadership or think the threat Ramirez and his men poses is too great to your safety, I invite you to leave. No repercussions. No hard feelings. However, if any one of you so much as thinks of stepping out of line and putting this club in further danger, I'll strip the motherfucking ink out of your backs right here and now." I can see the hairs on the back of his neck slowly rising. The silent pause that follows is uncomfortable to say the least. Half the Widow Makers are looking at their feet when Rebel continues. "And should any one of you so much as think about making life here difficult for Sophia, you're going to have to deal with me personally. Old or young. Man or woman. You've trusted me for the past five years, followed me through hell and back, so trust me now when I say this: you have *never* seen me pushed to my limit. Do *not* fucking test me. It will *not* end well."

SOPHIA

hen we get back to the cabin, Rebel puts me in his bed
and tells me he'll be back, and then I watch him through the
half open bathroom door as he strips down to his boxers and
methodically washes the blood from his body. He's constructed
beautifully, the planes of his muscles twisting and shifting in unison as
he moves carefully around the bathroom. I can tell his side is still
bothering him. And now he has two angry looking purple bruises
planted in the middle of his chest where the prongs of the Taser made
contact as well. There's a lot of grunting and wincing as he cleans
himself up. Sloane would tell him to sit his ass down so she could help
him, but Rebel...he probably wouldn't comply. He's fiercely proud. He's
used to this—I can tell. If I try and interfere, he'll probably shut down
and instead of making progress we'll be backtracking. I leave him to
clean his wound and replace his bandages himself. He throws back what
I'm assuming are more pain killers and antibiotics, and then he braces
against the counter and stares at himself in the mirror for what feels
like a very long time. He doesn't seem to like what he sees.

When he comes to bed, I'm still intimidated by his performance back
at the clubhouse. Intimidated enough that I pretend to be asleep. He

sees through the ruse, though, pulling me to him without fear of waking me. He doesn't say anything. He just strokes his hand over my hair, breathing deeply in the darkness, and I listen to his heart charging underneath his ribcage. He's running a fever, his skin burning against my cheek as we lay there. I wonder if he'll be a little better by the morning. Probably not. I mean, it's going to take longer than a few days to recover from a serious injury like that, especially if he keeps moving around, attacking people with baseball bats and getting shot by DEA agents. I get the impression that tomorrow will be more of the same, somehow.

It doesn't take long before Rebel's breathing evens out. I'm chasing sleep myself, but before it can claim me a thought strikes me. An unpleasant one. It takes me a moment to pluck up the courage to speak. When I do, my voice is nothing more than a whisper in the dark. "Rebel?"

"Mmm?

"That DEA agent? You think she'll come here? You think...you think she'll recognize me?"

He inhales, then rests his chin against the top of my head, the same way he did this morning when he comforted me. It all feels too familiar. Too safe. Too right. "Yeah," he whispers back. "She'll come here. She'll probably recognize you."

"And then what? What do I tell her?"

He's quiet. Too quiet. I already know I'm not going to like his response. "You tell her one of two things, Sophia. You tell her I kidnapped you and you've been held against your will for the past few weeks."

"Or?"

"Or you tell her you left Seattle of your own free will. That this is where you want to be. That this is your home now. Here with us."

77

It feels late when I wake up. Sunlight pours in through the window above the bed, warming my skin, though I'm cold. I've been used to half-surfacing from sleep throughout the night and feeling Rebel's body kicking out enough heat to warm me in the dead of winter, but now I can tell I'm alone. I don't open my eyes. I lie very still, listening. Sure enough, the sound of someone moving around at the other end of the room reaches me, confirming that Rebel's up and about. Slowly, carefully, I turn over and crack my eyelids, searching him out.

He's still in his boxers, standing in the open doorway of the cabin, with what looks like a notepad and paper in his hands. There's a small snow globe at his feet—a snow globe of Chicago's skyline. Back at his father's house in Alabama there were at least twenty more of them, from different cities all around the world, collected by his mother. The snow globe from Chicago is the only one he has here with him, though. Not for the first time, I wonder what makes that one in particular so special.

"Sleep okay?" Rebel asks. He hasn't turned around but he's figured out that I'm awake. I pull the covers up around my body a little closer, fighting the urge to hide completely.

"Yeah, I guess."

"Good." He pivots and freezes with the sunlight casting him into silhouette as he faces me, pen in one hand, paper in the other. He's so damn beautiful. Not jock pretty like Matt was. No, Rebel's body bears a striking similarity to a vase my mother keeps on her side table at home. Sloane and I were playing when we were kids, soccer inside the house, and we'd knocked the vase off the table. It had shattered into a thousand tiny pieces. Mom was devastated. It took Dad a solid three weeks to figure out where each tiny sliver of porcelain belonged and to glue it back into place. I think Mom loved the vase even more once Dad had finished the job. So much painstaking effort had gone into repairing it that it didn't matter to her if it was riddled with a spider web of fine chips and fractures. I have no idea who has spent so long over fixing all the injuries to Rebel's body—many people, I'm sure—but his body somehow seems more beautiful for all the scars and imperfections. Matt

78

would whine like a little bitch if he rolled an ankle during football practice. I'm yet to hear Rebel complain once about the fact that his belly was half-ripped open, or that he was shot up with thousands of volts of electricity.

I can just about make his features out as he gives me a grin that would take me out at the knees if I were standing. "You done, or should I come closer and give you a better look?" he asks softly. "You keep peering out of those covers at me and I might just come back to bed."

"That sounds like a threat."

"It is. And more. I'll make good on the promise I made you the other day, if you like?"

It takes me a second to remember what he's referring to. When I do, my cheeks feel like they're on fire. He's referring to making me come. Properly. Showing me that the female orgasm isn't just a myth. Holy shit...

Rebel stalks into the room like a panther, like now he's had to chance to think about making me scream and he's decided it's a really great idea. I have no idea if he's just trying to scare me or if this is something more. And I have no idea if I want it to be more. It makes me feel safe to pretend I don't want him, but it's exhausting and I've never been good at lying. Even to myself.

Truth is, I'm addicted to the man.

I should hate him. I should be scared of him. I shouldn't want him anywhere near me, and yet...

"You can do what you want," I whisper. "You normally do."

He gives me a smirk. "Well, well. I do believe that wasn't a no." He walks back into the cabin, holding his torso rigid—I can see he's already freshly dressed his wounds again this morning—as though he's trying not to pull his stitches. I never thought I'd be the kind of person to look at a man like this. Like I'm hungry for him. It's embarrassing, but it's also freeing in some weird way, too. Sex has never been a big deal for me. It's never played a huge role in my life. Ever since Matt and I got together, I assumed I just had a low sex drive and that was okay because he was always pretty vanilla about things and would finish up quickly anyway. But now... now I know my sex drive isn't low. It's just been dormant, laying in wait for the right person to come and awaken it. As I lay in Rebel's bed, rubbing my feet together, trying not to think about the building pressure between my legs or the wicked look that's spreading across his face, I'm pretty sure I've found that person. Or rather he found me.

"I'm just saying. Would it matter even if I did say no? You seem to get your own way most of the time, regardless of what anyone else has planned."

He stops dead in his tracks. "Not all the time, Soph. Not with this. You think I'd force you to fuck me?" He's lost that playful air to him. It's vanished in a puff of smoke. Instead, he looks...hurt?

"No. No, that's not what I meant. I...I just—"

"Think that I would coerce you in some way?" He frowns deeply, those blue eyes of his clouding over. It takes less than the space of a heartbeat to realize that I've said the wrong thing. I regret opening my mouth instantly. I should have thought.

"No. I don't think you would ever coerce me. I really don't. I shouldn't have said that. You just...you make me feel like I'm...out of control."

"You are *always* in control, Soph. *Always*. If you haven't figured it out yet, I'm at your disposal, day or night. My club members step out of line and they'll know about it, but you can pretty much get away with murder. I'm not a fan of games, Sophia. I've kept my mouth shut since Alabama because you looked terrified at the time, but I told you back in that hallway that you were mine for as long as you wanted to be. *And I was yours.* You didn't take my hand. You were scared by the idea of it, I know. But it's still true. That hasn't changed. As long as you're here, with me, you have nothing to be afraid of. And that includes me."

I can't think of the right thing to say. When he looks at me the way he's looking at me right now, I can't think straight at the best of times. But coupled with the intensity in his voice and the way my body has just responded to his words, I don't have a hope in hell of forming a coherent sentence.

He sighs, throwing the notepad and pen down on the end of the bed.

"I'm going to figure out how to shower with all of these bandages. You can get some more sleep if you like." He turns and heads for the bathroom door.

"Rebel, wait!"

He does. Glancing over his shoulder at me, he waits for me to speak. Me being me, I'm hoping that he'll let me off, cut me some slack, not make me say it, but of course he's him and that's not how this thing works. I'm learning that slowly. Frustration courses through my veins. Why can't he be a gentleman about this and just come get into bed with me? Rebel shakes his head, a small, barely-there smile twitching at the corners of his mouth.

"Be brave, sugar. I know you are. You just gotta prove it," he says softly.

In a million other situations, I'd get stubborn on his ass. I'd slump down in the bed, hiding under the covers, and I'd let him go take his shower, refusing to step up to the plate. This is different, though. If I did that right now, I wouldn't be winning. I'd be losing, big time. I let out a shaky breath, pulling myself up a little in the bed. "All right, fine. I don't want you to go for a shower. I want you to stay here. With me."

"Oh? And why would that be?"

I could kick him in the shins for being so quietly smug, but it's actually a very sexy look on him. He pulls it off well enough for me to be squirming in the bed as he slowly faces me again. "You know why," I tell him.

"You have to tell me."

"Because..."

"Because?" He takes another step closer to the bed.

"Because...I want you."

A bright fire burns in Rebel's eyes. "How?"

"I want to feel you on top of me, pushing my legs apart, pushing your way inside me. I want to get lost in you."

"You want me to fuck you hard or slow, Soph?" He seems fascinated by the words I'm forcing out of my mouth. He seems to be savoring every last one. He stares at my mouth as he stalks purposefully toward the bed.

"Slow," I whisper. "I want you to fuck me slow. I want to feel every last movement. Every last second that you're inside me. I want to feel your arms tight around me, so I can barely breathe. I want to forget."

He gives me a sharp look. "Forget about what? Bron? Dela Vega?"

Slowly, so slowly, I shake my head. Why is this so damn hard to say? I've come this far now—the rest of it should be easy. It isn't, though. Opening my mouth, telling him what I want, is the hardest thing in the world. I've climbed mountains and overcome so many ridiculous obstacles recently, and yet *this* is where I flounder—here, trying to tell him the truth. He makes me feel small. Vulnerable. *Afraid.* "No," I say. "Not about them. I want to forget where you begin and I end. I want to forget what it feels like to exist without you. I don't want to dance around this anymore. I was scared back in Alabama, you're right. But now the only thing that scares me? The only thing that scares me is *not* being with you."

As he rushes the last few steps to the bed, Rebel doesn't seem to care about his injuries anymore. I think he's going to jump on me, rip the covers from my body and devour me, but he doesn't. He kneels on the bed, sitting back on his heels and bracing his hands on his thighs, staring at me, his chest rising and falling quickly. "You have no idea..." he growls. "You have no idea what I want to do to you, Sophia. But you're about to find out. Are you ready? Do I have your consent?"

Panic grips me, but I force myself to let go of it. In the past I'd have grabbed hold of this fear with two hands and refused to let go, giving myself an excuse to back out of whatever situation I found intimidating. I can't afford to be that way, though. Not if I want to find out where all of this leads. Despite every single warning bell going off in my head, that's exactly what I want. I nod, slowly drawing in a deep breath. "Yes. Yes, you have my consent."

Rebel eyes glitter. I can see his intention in them, and it's both thrilling and frightening at the same time. I know he's going to come for me now, but knowing it and seeing it happen are two very different things. When he bends slowly, placing both hands on the bed in front of him, and begins making his way closer, I feel like I'm about to pass out.

"You want me to come inside you, Sophia?" he says, his voice a low, dangerous rumble in the back of his throat.

"Yes."

"Good girl." He moves so he can peel back the comforter that's still covering me, and then he takes a second to inspect the length of my naked legs. The t-shirt I'm wearing seems really damn short all of a sudden. As if that bothers Rebel, though. He gently makes contact with my skin, running his hands lightly up the outsides of my thighs. I break out in goose bumps at his touch, sending violent shivers chasing through me. When his hands hit the hem of the t-shirt I'm wearing, he fingers the material, following the stitching along the hem until his hands meet in the middle. I know things are about to get crazy when his eyes meet mine and I can see the lust burning in them. "You know you should be naked right now?" he says. I'm going to respond, going to tell him that I want to be, but I'm not given the opportunity. Rebel grips the bottom of the t-shirt in both hands and pulls, splitting the material right up the middle.

The action is violent and makes me jump, but he doesn't hurt me. The t-shirt's in ruins, though. Completely unsalvageable. It's kind of ridiculous that I've been wearing a shirt that says, *It's Not Going To Suck Itself* anyway. Rebel removes the rest of the shirt from my body with persuasive hands, but he doesn't touch my naked breasts. Doesn't even glance at the rest of my bare flesh. His eyes remain locked onto mine, his breathing growing faster and faster. His skin is still boiling hot. He's still feverish, though he doesn't seem likely to let that hinder him in his current activity. Once I'm naked and lying on the bed in front of him, Rebel carefully positions himself in between my legs, kneeling over me.

"You're a problem, Sophia," he tells me. "You're like the most complex, infuriating math problem I've ever attempted."

I curve an eyebrow at him, trying not to look at his increasingly noticeable hard-on. I smile a little, determined not to hide my body from him, even though the effort is killing me. "More complicated than Legendre's Conjecture?" I ask.

Rebel laughs. I could be wrong, but I get the impression he's a little impressed. "You remember what it's called, huh?"

"What it's called, yes. If you asked me to draw it out, that might be a problem, though."

"Oh, well, we can solve that." He leans back and grabs the pen he was using before, pulling the cap off with his teeth. How such an action can be sexy, I have no idea, but he manages it. It's hot as hell, in fact. He spits out the cap and then holds up the pen—a blue sharpie—giving me a questioning look. "You ready for me to get mathematical on you, sugar?"

"You want to scribble messy equations all over my body?"

When he opens his mouth, he's switched on the Alabama charm. "Why, I'm a tattoo artist. I ain't never made a mess on nobody's skin. And I sure as hell ain't ever *scribbled* on anyone, either. Now, please be so kind as to oblige me while I create a work of art on your already perfect body, darlin'."

The southern accent has always made me cringe, but when Rebel speaks slow and deep the way he just did, I find myself reacting very differently. Very differently indeed. I want to press my knees together again, to stem the building need I'm experiencing, but I can't because he's still kneeling in between my legs.

I am frozen marble as he takes the tip of the sharpie and begins to slowly draw on my hipbone. From there, he travels upward toward my belly button in an arcing beautiful cursive that incorporates long, sweeping blue lines and curlicues that dip down low onto my stomach. He doesn't rush. He takes his time. I feel every hot breath he takes as he works over me, frowning in concentration.

I have no idea what true values the numbers or shapes represent as he marks them onto me, but he was right; this isn't a scribble, and it's sure as hell not messy. It's remarkable. He works for another fifteen minutes, his movements becoming slower, more considered, as the seconds tick by. My nerve endings jump every time tip of the pen makes contact. My heart races a little faster every time he exhales over the expanse of my bare skin. Eventually, I realize he's noticed my involuntary reactions and he's taking his time with me on purpose, drawing this out, making it last longer.

His pen travels down, down, down, and I clear my throat. When he looks up, his face is already lit with a savage grin that I haven't been able to see until now. "Little uncomfortable?" he asks.

"Just wondering if you're going to color me in entirely is all."

He laughs again. "I think you'd look great as a smurf. I've only just discovered how hot it is to watch you jump and squirm when I do this. It's made my cock rock solid, Soph. All I can think about is how beautiful you'd look if I were tattooing you for real and this was a gun in my hand. I think watching you writhe around while you were getting inked would have me coming in a heart beat."

A cold, strange shudder runs through my body—half dread, half excitement. There were lots of girls at school who had tattoos all over their bodies, some of which were real works of art. I never looked at them and thought, 'yeah, that's me,' though. I never planned out what I would look like if I were to have some serious ink going on. It never even crossed my mind, mainly because I knew what my father would say if I came home with a tattoo. He'd lose his freaking mind.

"I'm not letting you tattoo me," I tell him. "No way in hell."

"Why?" Rebel puts the cap back on the pen and tosses it over his shoulder, looking devious. "Afraid?"

"Is this the part where you tell me I'm a chicken and it wouldn't hurt?"

"Oh, no. It can hurt like a bitch, sugar." Slowly, he ducks down and licks the skin just above my belly button, never taking his eyes off me. "It's just that some pleasures are worth the pain. You wouldn't know about that, I'm sure. I'll show you if you like?"

I've never wanted anything as much as I want him now. I think he can see that in my eyes, because he smiles. "Are you wet yet, Sophia?" he whispers. "If you're not ready for me, I can always color you in some more."

I nod, struggling to keep my hands still beside me. It's as though they have a mind of their own. I want to touch him. I want to bury my hands in his hair. I want to trace my fingers over the deep purple bruises on his chest, and then I want to gently kiss both of them. I imagine what his skin would taste like if I licked him the same way he just licked me, and my hands curl into fists. "No more coloring," I whisper.

"As you wish." Rebel kisses my body, sending wave after wave of pleasure soaring through me as he moves from the very start of the equation he's just drawn on my hip, up, up, up my ribcage, until he reaches my left breast. It's far from cold in the cabin, but my nipples have tightened to almost painful proportions already. It's cruel, cruel torture when he takes my nipple into his mouth and gently sucks, trailing his tongue over my sensitive flesh, flicking it with the tip of his tongue.

"Oh...*oh my god.*"

He sucks harder, and my back arches off the bed, curving into his body. I can feel how badly he wants me now. I've already seen how big he's gotten but to feel his erection digging into my belly makes this whole situation seem more...I don't know. Surreal in some ways? Because this isn't me. I'm not the girl who grinds her hips up against a guy I barely know as he teases my nipples with his fingers and his mouth.

Rebel palms my right breast with his free hand, kneading lightly, breathing hard down his nose. Every single muscle in his body is tight and tense as he slowly starts to rock against me, pressing his cock against my pussy, creating the most amazing friction. I forget I'm meant to be a timid mouse in this situation.

I wrap my arms around his neck, pulling him closer to me. Rebel groans as he continues to grind his body against mine, and the sound of his pleasure sends a sharp, demanding shockwave of need through me. I want to hear him make that sound again. I want him to be inside me when he does. My hands are working quickly, then, pulling at the waistband of his boxers.

Rebel takes hold of my left hand first and then the other, pinning them above my head. "I thought you wanted this slow."

"I do."

"Then don't tempt me."

He slides down my body, and then he's pulling my legs apart even further, making a pleased humming sound at the back of his throat as he stares at my pussy. If I weren't so turned on, I'd probably be cringing. Instead I'm biting on my bottom lip like a character out of some trashy romance novel, feeling electrified by the way his eyes travel so slowly over me.

"You want my tongue, sugar?" he growls.

"Yes. Yes, I want it," I pant. "*Please.*"

He chuckles under his breath, running his hands down the insides of my thighs. "You're incredible," he tells me. "Just...fucking...incredible." When he dips and teases his tongue over my clit, my head starts spinning. I have no idea how guys learn how to give head, but Matt could have done with some lessons from the school Rebel attended. He knows exactly what to do to set off those fireworks in my brain. It occurs to me that he's probably so good at it because he's had years and years of practice with god knows how many women, but the thought is fleeting. Neither my body nor my mind will allow me to think about things like that right now. Not when I could be floating on this cloud, feeling like the tether holding me to this earth could snap any second and I could drown in nothingness. It's what I want. No, it's what I *need.*

Rebel has me on the brink of coming and he must know it. Just as it feels like I'm climbing, lifting, rising to the top of some giant roller-coaster, he slides his index finger and his middle finger inside me and every last synapse in my brain starts firing.

"Jesus, you really do taste like sugar," he groans. "I can't get enough of you." He only has to pump his fingers into three or four more times before he pushes me over the edge and I plummet, heart hammering, hands clinging to the sheets, vision narrowing and my ears ringing.

It takes me a moment to realize my thighs are locked tight around Rebel's head and his tongue is still working over my clitoris, stretching out the end of my orgasm, making the muscles in my stomach and the backs of my legs twitch and flex.

"Oh, shit. Stop, stop. *Please*! Stop!" I'm laughing uncontrollably, but it's manic, pleading. He's driving me crazy. I'm way too sensitive for him to carry on. He stops, rocking back on his heels, a very smug smile spreading across his face.

"You taste like candy," he says, as he gets up off the bed and finally removes his boxer shorts. I've been waiting for this for a long time. Sure, we had sex in the hallway at his dad's place, and, yes, we did it again the other night, but I've never *seen* him. Never had the chance to check out what he's got going on down there. Rebel seems to know that I want to see him properly. He doesn't rush back onto the bed. He stands, shoulders back, covered in bruises, favoring his good side, but he doesn't hide his cock. If anything, he's pretty damn proud of it as he remains frozen to the spot, allowing me to get a good look. And he has every right to be proud. Matt was pretty straight laced, but he did like to watch porn with me every once in a while. Rebel easily rivals any of the guys we saw in those 'movies.' His cock is perfection. It's actually *beautiful.* That seems like a strange thought to have about a penis, but it's true. It makes me want to do weird things...like take a plaster cast of it and make myself a personalized Rebel dildo that I can tease myself with it when he's not around.

"I take it you like what you see?" he asks. "You've got this look on your face. Somewhere between complete carnal lust and overwhelming relief."

I laugh. "Overwhelming relief?"

He nods, climbing back up onto the bed, back up onto me. "Yes. Like you thought I somehow tricked you before and I was going to have a micro-dick."

More laughter, though it's strained now. I can feel him between my legs, pressing against the entrance to my pussy. If he so much as takes a deep breath, he'll be inside me. And god, I want that. "I'm not...sizeist," I tell him.

"Doesn't matter." Rebel pushes forward just the tiniest little bit, but the feeling of him entering me makes me dizzy in the best possible way. "Even if I had a two inch cocktail sausage for a dick, I could still make you come with it. I could still make you scream my fucking name. I know what I'm doing, sugar, and it makes me seriously fucking hard to bring you pleasure. Now, are you ready for me to make you come?"

His gaze penetrates me deep. The heat from his body on top of me is making my head spin. "I'm ready," I tell him. And he pushes into me, slowly, with purpose, staring me in the eye, his arms braced either side of my head as he sinks deeper and deeper. He feels...he feels *amazing*. Before, things have always felt amazing, but this is something else entirely. He doesn't pull back straight away; he holds himself in place, holding me in his gaze, and it feels like something clicks. That sounds ridiculous, but it's true. It feels like the last tiny shred of resistance I may have habored concerning this man is gone, banished, destroyed, and now I'm screwed. I won't be able to hold myself back anymore.

I'm surprised by the look in Rebel's eyes when he finally pulls back, drawing out of me so he can repeat the motion. He looks surprised. A little shocked even? He shakes his head, grinning a little, and then he really takes my breath away. He supports himself with one hand, and then cups my face with the other, bringing his lips down on mine. Kissing him isn't something I've daydreamed about. I haven't allowed the thought to cross my mind. We kissed back at his father's place, but we were both desperate then, fighting to control ourselves. We were ripping and tearing at each other like wild animals. Those kisses were intense and powerful, but our mouths were crashing together, devouring one another. Now, the way he kisses me is purposeful and direct. His mouth is soft on mine, but he's in control. Lowering his full weight on top of me, he leans on his elbows, which frees up his other hand to brush the hair back out of my face, trace his fingers across the line of my cheekbone, my jaw, my temple. He moves slow just like I asked him to, but he makes sure he's deep inside me each time before he draws away. I move with him, feeling trapped and safe beneath him at the same time, both scared and whole.

This is nothing like the encounters we've shared before. This feels honest. Like a promise somehow. He holds onto me so tight as he fucks me. It's not long before both of us are shaking with the effort of keeping ourselves together. I lock my legs around his waist and we come at the same time, Rebel growling into my neck, crushing me to him as he climaxes.

We lay together, panting, unable to move as the early morning sunshine shines down on our bodies, and I realize that he gave me what I asked of him. He made me forget. He made me forget where he began and I ended.

And it feels perfect.

REBEL

Burying a body's never fun. When you're only burying part of it, it's even less fun. Back in Afghanistan, my boy and I buried fucking dismembered arms and legs all the time. The Marine Corps were pretty diligent about making sure the pieces of people they were sending back to the States all belonged to the same body, but I'm guessing often times DNA got a little fused together. Not a pleasant thought. Really fucked up, in fact. I made sure the army knew I didn't want to be flown back to Alabama if I was K.I.A. Told them I wanted to be cremated and scattered to the four winds from a rooftop in Kabul. Last thing I ever wanted to do was give my asshole father the pleasure of interring me in the Aubertin family mausoleum instead of burying me with my brothers in a military cemetery. He didn't respect the time I spent overseas. He would have stuck me in the cheapest pine box he could find, left me on the bottom shelf underneath my mother's dusty coffin, blinked a couple of times at what remained of his only son, then casually locked the door. He wouldn't have returned until it was time for his own empty husk to be shelved and forgotten about, too.

Motherfucker.

Burying Bron is a different affair entirely. I'm sick to my stomach and in pain, but I figure if I have enough energy to make Sophia come then it's only right that I have the energy to go out into the desert and dig a grave with Brassic.

As I thrust the shovel into the sun-baked dirt three miles south of the Widow Makers' compound, sweat running in rivers down my back, running into my eyes, salt in my mouth, my head spinning just enough to let me know this is a really bad idea, I'm trying not to think about Sophia. I'm trying not to think about how edge-of-a-knife this whole thing is. I'm ready to burn the whole fucking world down for this girl. I wonder if she knows that? I wonder if she knows how many people I'd tear limb from limb myself in order to keep her safe.

I'm not like her, though. I don't wear every single thought I have on my face, or in my body language. I keep things close to my chest. It's the only way I've survived this world for so long.

Other members of the club have survived by alternative means. Cade's stone cold like me, but his temper is legendary. People don't fuck with him, because they know the consequences will be dire to say the fucking least. Shay uses her body to protect herself. She'll make you think you're about to get the ride of our life, when in actual fact you're about to get a stiletto blade slipped through your eardrum and into your gray matter without a by your leave. She really is a true widow maker. The guy I'm digging this grave with, Brassic, is our resident bomb maker. He won't hurt you with his fists. He'll hurt you with a pound of C4 and a remote detonator while he's a mile away slamming back a shot of whiskey.

He doesn't talk while we dig. Neither of us do. He's angry that I wouldn't let him go after the guy who killed his best friend's girl last night when his rage was peaking, but he won't show it openly. Good thing for him, too. I'm not in the mood to be questioned. My side is killing me, and all I can think about as our shovels make dry, *shink, shink, shink* sounds in the dirt is that I somehow have to fix this fucking Ramirez mess under the noses of the DEA. Highly fucking inconvenient.

"We're digging this hole for the wrong person, you realize," Brassic says. It's the first thing he's said since we started working, and it's so true it makes my head pound.

"I do know."

Brassic grunts. He's slick with sweat like I am, except the vast expanse of his back bears the Widow Makers' club badge instead of the Virgin Mary that I have inked into my skin. She was my first tattoo, my holy lady. The space had already been taken by the time I started the Widow Makers, and besides, it's better for me not to have any club markings. There are times when I need to go places, see and do things that I wouldn't be able to if people suspected I had affiliations to a biker gang. In those instances, if they knew I was the *president* of a biker gang, I'd be murdered on the spot.

"So when, then?" Brassic asks. He sounds tired; I know for a fact he was up all night with Keeler, drinking and smashing the shit out of the workshop in one of the outhouses, so his head must be killing him.

"Soon. Really soon, man," I tell him.

"And you'll give me free rein?"

I mop my brow, eyes still stinging, my head swimming, and I say, "Buddy, when this thing goes down, you don't need to worry. You can turn the bastard into red mist and I will thank you for it."

In the distance, thick plumes of dust billow up into pale, washed out blue of the sky overhead. Cars. Three of them. I can't see what kind they are or who is driving them, but they're traveling fast.

We walked out here to clear our heads. We fucking walked. Brassic turns giving me a concerned look. "We need to get back?" he asks.

I have a sick, anxious feeling in the pit of my stomach as I watch those cars speeding toward the distant compound. "Yeah. Yeah, man. We need to get back. *Now.*"

SOPHIA

I've never noticed that Cade has a slight limp before. I notice it well enough when he's charging across the compound toward me like a crazy person, though. He favors his left side, skipping his right foot behind him ever so slightly as he charges in my direction with a stony expression on his face. I can feel the worry pouring off him when he pitches up in front of me.

"You should get back up to the cabin, Soph."

"Why?" No way am I going back to the cabin. I have no specific reason for being in the courtyard outside the clubhouse but I'll be damned if I'm being sent away again already. I am sick of being cooped up. Sick of feeling a prisoner. Cade must see me bristle; he blows out an exasperated breath, holding his hands up in the air.

"We got visitors, okay. And not the nice kind. Better you aren't here for it," he says.

I feel like being stubborn some more, but the look on his face tells me that might not be wise. "Who is it?" I ask.

"Don't know. Not DEA, but still... no one good. C'mon. Get back up the hill. *Please.* Jamie will kill me if I let anything happen to you."

He looks genuinely concerned. Out of the corner of my eye, the woman with pink hair from last night, Shay, emerges from the club-house, pulling on a dirty white t-shirt over her florescent pink bra. Classy. She shoots me the foulest look ever, and then frowns as she squints into the distance beyond the compound gates. When I follow her gaze, I see what she sees: tall columns of dust, red and brown, growing closer and closer. Too close, it would seem. The hood of a black car is visible, only meters away from the gates, but there are more behind, following.

"Shit," Cade hisses. The first black car screeches to a halt, kicking up more dust and debris as it almost crashes into the gates. The sound of hot metal ticking reaches us, and then the loud *crack!* of a gun being fired. Sounds like it came from inside the car. I can just make out the shape of a figure slumping forward in the driver's seat, and then the car's horn starts screaming, blaring out obnoxious sound into the quiet.

"Ah, sweet Jesus." Cade steps to the right, blocking me from view of the car. He sends Shay a sharp look that she returns, arms folded across her chest. "Make sure this one doesn't come to any harm," he tells her.

She scowls and then spits on the ground at her feet. "Rebel said not to threaten her. Didn't say nothing about *protecting* her."

Cade pivots on the balls of his feet and begins marching toward her. He looks like he's about to tear her head from her shoulders. She holds up her hands, taking a step back, eyes wide. "All right, all right! Fuck, man, it was a joke."

Cade's not in the mood for jokes, though. "Just do as you're fucking told, Shay."

A high pitched screaming joins in the sound of the car horn, and suddenly there are people climbing out of the first car while a second and a third pull up alongside the first, blocking the gate to the compound entirely. I couldn't see it before, but all three vehicles are completely riddled with bullet holes.

A tall, leggy blonde in a tight black dress and red stilettos emerges from the first car. She looks like a wild animal, dark eyes round and filled with madness. As soon as she's on her feet, she turns and unceremoniously drags the lifeless body of a huge man out of the car behind her. He looks like he's half dead; given the amount of blood spattering the woman's arms and legs, he could actually be all-the-way dead.

Shay's mouth hangs open, surprise taking over her features. "Is that...?"

"Maria Rosa?" Cade finishes. "Yeah. Yeah, it is."

It takes me a second to remember who this woman is. I've met so many new people and been introduced to so many new threats recently that this recalling where Maria Rosa fits in takes a beat. I get there fairly quickly, though. Maria Rosa. What was it Carnie called her the day the police came to search the compound? That's right...the Bitch of Columbia. The head of the Desolladors Cartel—the woman who tried to frame Rebel by sending men in Widow Makers cuts into a grocery store in Hollywood and mowing down women and children.

"What the fuck is she doing here?" I whisper this under my breath, unable to give force to my words. I'm too disbelieving, too stunned, too completely horrified to grasp what I'm seeing in front of me.

"I don't know," Cade replies. "But it looks as though, as per usual, the psycho bitch has brought trouble with her."

"Help me! *SOMEBODY HELP ME!*" Maria Rosa topples to the ground, tripping on her own heels as she tries to drag the extremely heavy looking body toward the gates. She spins around, fury and panic lighting up her face. She sees the man standing next to me and the panic vanishes, completely replaced by anger. "What the fuck is wrong with you? Get over here, Cade. Get over here and fucking help me."

More people pour out of the cars—all men in black suits and white shirts with guns in their hands—but Cade remains utterly still. His eyes look cold. Dead, almost. "You really are insane if you think for one second you're getting through those gates, darlin'."

Maria Rosa lets go of the man's arm and stalks up to the metal railings of the gate, a wicked snarl twisting her features. I can tell that she's a beautiful woman usually, but at the moment she looks like medusa—her hair is everywhere, her eyeliner smudged down her face, bright red lipstick smeared. She's hysterical, and from what I can tell about to get much, much worse.

"You let me through these gates, Cade," she snaps. "Let me through, or I'll make sure this one finds his way inside all by himself. He's been telling me all about how he'd like to fuck the pretty little thing you have hiding in your shadow."

I only put two and two together and realize she's talking about me when she jerks her head at one of her men and Raphael Dela Vega appears. He strains against the taller, broader man holding onto him, desperately trying to get free. I spot the crude spider tattoo on his face and it all comes rushing back to me—him telling me how he was going to rape and kill my mother and sister right in front of me. I feel dizzy, like I'm about to pass out. He's haunted my dreams, but this is the first time I've laid eyes on him since the night Rebel bought me. I've tried to pretend he doesn't exist, tried to pretend he's dead somehow, that Hector tired of him and got rid of him, but no. Here he is in all his savage glory, only twenty feet away from where I'm standing now. And Maria Rosa's threatening to set him free on our doorstep. Irrational as it may be, I'm terrified. Since the gunshots, car horn and Maria Rosa's screaming took place, twenty Widow Makers have materialized out of the compound buildings, all holding guns, all ready to put a bullet in this woman's head for fucking with their club name. I *know* they aren't going to let Raphael anywhere near me, but still... I can feel his eyes crawling all over my skin, can sense the dark things he wants to do to me, and it makes my heart squeeze in my chest.

"Shoot them all," Shay says. "We don't need any of them alive. Just fucking kill them all."

For the first time since I've met the woman, I finally find myself agreeing with something that's come out of her mouth. Less than a second after I think this, the weight of that hits me in the gut like a battering ram. Kill them all. I want them all dead. There are perhaps eleven people on the other side of the gate including Maria Rosa and Raphael, and I just agreed that I wanted them all dead.

Who am I becoming?

They're drug dealers, murders, human traffickers and rapists. If my father were here, he would forgive them of their sins and invite them inside so he could help their wounded. I want to double chain the gate, douse the bastards in petrol and strike a match.

I would watch them burn.

Maria Rosa snatches a gun from the guy standing closest to her and holds it up, aiming though the bars of the gate at Cade. "If you kill us," she hisses, "I won't be able to tell you what Ramirez has planned for you, will I?"

I'm still all for killing her, but Cade falters. Shay cocks a mean looking gun, holding it up with both hands as she moves closer to Cade. "She's bluffing. She doesn't know anything about Ramirez. Let me put a fucking bullet between her eyes, man."

"You think Rebel would do that?" he asks.

Shay's determination flickers, only for a second. Only for the briefest of pauses. It's enough for Cade, though. "Exactly. He'd want to know what she knows first. And *then* he'd kill her."

I don't like his tone of voice at all. It sounds for all the world like he's about to do as she asks. "You are *not* going to let her in here, right?" It seems like sheer madness that he would even consider such a thing, and yet he gives me a tight-lipped smile and starts walking toward the gate.

"You, Rico, *him*,"—he points at the guy holding onto Raphael—"and Hector's guy. That's it. Everyone else needs to get gone. Then you can come in."

"You're crazy!" Maria Rosa laughs scornfully. "I'm not walking into the lion's den with only one able-bodied guard. You must think I'm stupid."

"No, I think you're desperate otherwise you wouldn't have come here. The choice is yours, Mother."

Mother? My head is spinning. Why the hell would he call her that? It makes no sense. No one else seems to find it strange, though. The Widow Makers surrounding me are all wearing severe expressions, hands resting on their guns, some blatantly holding them out like Shay. I'm the only one who looks lost, I'm sure. Cade shrugs, smiling in a dramatic, all of a sudden way that is totally out of place.

"When you make up your mind, you let me know, okay? Meantime, I'll be in the clubhouse drinking a cold one." He begins to turn around, turning his back on the crazed woman on the other side of the gate, but she starts screaming again.

"*¡Te odio! usted es un enfermo, el mal hijo de puta!*"

Cade faces her again, grinning. "Oh, don't worry, Mother. I hate you, too."

There's pure murder in her eyes when she lowers her gun. "Fine. Just the four of us. But trust me...if you value your life and the lives of your precious Widow Makers, you won't lay a finger on me or mine."

Cade draws an ex over his chest. "Cross my heart and hope to die."

"I've hoped you would die many times over already, *cabron*."

"Likewise." Cade stares at her until she loses patience and starts barking at her men in Spanish, presumably telling them to leave. They look unsure at first, and then afraid as she gets angrier and angrier. Eventually seven other men climb into two of the cars, start the engines and leave.

"There. Are you happy now? Rico is *dying*, motherfucker. Let us inside."

I have no idea who this Rico guy is, but he sure as hell seems important to Maria Rosa. Cade grunts, still grinning, though the humor has vanished from his face. He looks like he's grimacing as he slowly strolls to the compound gate and punches a code into the keypad to the left. The metal screeches as the gates swing open and then Maria Rosa is charging into the compound, holding up her gun. She marches straight up to Cade and presses the gleaming metal directly against his heart.

"You'd better fix him," she spits. "You'd better fix him, or there will be consequences, asshole."

I'd be curious to see what these consequences are, now that twenty angry Widow Makers surround her. Cade says something, but I don't really hear it, though. The two of them talk, anger and antagonism lacing their voices, and I stare at Raphael, feeling panic rising in the back of my throat. He's still being restrained, though the evil motherfucker isn't struggling anymore. He's staring right back at me, unblinking, apparently unfazed by the situation he finds himself in. He seems only intent on one thing: *me*. And the look in his eyes is enough to make the blood run cold in my veins.

"Well? Sophia? Can you do it?"

"Huh?" I tear my gaze from Raphael, shaking, to find that Cade has moved again and he's standing beside me. His eyebrows are raised in question. "What?" I ask.

"Can you take a look at the guy? You're studying medicine, right?"

I just look at him blankly. He can't...he can't actually be serious. Can he? "What? *No!* I study *psychology*."

Cade laughs like this is the funniest thing ever. He turns around, throwing his hands up in the air. "Well, there you have it. No doctors here, Mother. Sorry." He doesn't sound sorry. Not even a little. "I mean," he continues. "I can pull a slug out of him, but I can't guarantee I won't do more damage than good. He looks like he's on the way out, darlin'."

Maria Rosa sends him an icy stare. And then she turns it on me. "You're lying," she informs me. "You *are* a doctor."

"I'm not." I'm really damn glad none of these people know my father or my sister are actually doctors. They would probably assume I know what I'm doing by association or something. Turns out Maria Rosa doesn't need such information to make calls like that, though. "Bullshit. You can save him." She sounds like she's determined to make this the truth by sheer force of will. She's mad. I'm convinced of that fact when she turns her gun on me and removes the safety. "Get over here," she commands. "Get the bullet out of him and sew him up. You can do it."

"I—" I shake my head, not quite sure what to do. "I have no surgical experience. I'll kill him."

"Oh, no, princess. You kill him, and I kill you. I don't think you want that. You want to die?"

"Of course not."

"Then get over here and fix him!"

I can see that the man on the ground by the gate, Rico, is beyond saving. His lips and eyelids are blue, which I'm educated enough to know means he stopped breathing some time ago. I'm betting that if I walk over there and place my fingertips against his neck, I'm not going to find a pulse. I'm also betting Maria Rosa does not want to hear that, though. She seems like she's on the brink of a complete meltdown.

"I don't have any equipment. I'd need a sterile room, and surgical tools. I—I don't even have a needle and thread, let alone forceps. You do know what a psychologist is, right?"

Maria Rosa doesn't answer. She moves in a flash of tight Versace and highly impractical Manolos, and suddenly she has me by the hair. Both Cade and Shay move at the same time, trying to put themselves in between me and the woman, but Maria Rosa has a firm grip on me; my hair feels like it's about to be torn out at the roots.

"For fuck's sake," Cade groans under his breath. "If you really wanna piss Rebel off, you're doing a stellar job."

"Do I look like I give a fuck about Rebel?" Maria Rosa spits. "I only care about Rico." She proceeds to drag me toward Rico's body, jabbing me every few paces with what I'm assuming it the barrel of her gun. Raphael starts laughing in that rattling, weird, unnerving way of his. His cackling bounces around the compound courtyard like a mocking bird call. He stops laughing as I pass him to say, "I hope you're ready, slut. I'll be skull fucking you before the end of the night."

Anger rolls through me. I want to punch this woman in the ribcage for handling me like I'm shit, for bring that man in such close proximity of me, but I know she won't hesitate to shoot if I piss her off.

The Widow Makers all move in unison, crowding in around, all just as angry as I am. They may not know me or like me, but they love Rebel. As far as they are concerned, I am his property and Maria Rosa should not be interfering with me in any way.

Cade is beginning to look seriously worried. Maria Rosa shoves me forward roughly, and I fall to my knees beside Rico. My heart is charging so hard, I can hear my blood pumping in my own ears. The sound becomes a deafening roar when I feel the muzzle of the gun pressing into the back of my head.

This is not good. This is not good at all. I have no way of saving this man. I have no clue what I'm doing. Now that I'm closer I can see the bullet hole in his stomach, though, can see that someone has ineffectually tried to stem the flow of blood by ramming a black silk scarf into the wound. Right into it, like that was the best option available to them. Even I know that was a bad idea. That scarf has got all kinds of bacteria all over it, and now that bacteria is happily breeding away inside the torn up vital organs of a dying man.

"Begin," Maria Rosa commands.

"I told you, I don't have any instruments."

She crouches down beside me, craning her face into mine, baring her teeth so that she's showing gum. "*Use. Your. Fingers.*"

"I am not sticking my fingers inside his body. No way!"

Pain comes, then—a sharp, piercing pain at the back of my head. My vision dances, pinpricks of light bursting everywhere, but I don't lose consciousness. I do fall forward, though—my hands land right on Rico's torso. The man's eyes flicker open, and he gasps soundlessly for oxygen once, twice, and then his eyes roll back in his head. He starts to convulse, pink foam pouring out of his mouth.

"Ahhhh, Mother, the bitch killed him," Raphael laughs. "She's trouble. I told you, no?"

Maria Rosa lets out an anguished squeal. I look up, and see that she's hitting herself in the side of the head with her gun, pulling on her own hair. Tears tremble on the ends of her eyelashes, ready to fall any second. "He's not dead. You check him. Check his pulse," she growls.

I do check his pulse. It's thready and weak, but I can feel the irregular twitch of his heart beneath the pads of my fingers. Thank fuck for that. "He's not dead," I say. I hate how my voice shakes. I hate that I'm afraid right now, but it can't be helped. I keep finding myself in these situations. If I don't get shot in the back of the head in a couple of minutes and my brains aren't splattered all over Rico and the dirt and everywhere else in between, maybe I'll be less frightened the next time this happens. *Maybe.*

Maria Rosa grinds her teeth together, repositioning her gun in her hands again. "Okay. Now you get that bullet out of him, bitch, or I'm going put three in you. Do you hear me?" she screams.

I look from her to Cade and back again. Cade has his gun in his hands pointing it at Maria Rosa, but he looks torn. "I could shoot her if you want, Soph. I can't guarantee she won't shoot you first, though. It's your call. What do you want me to do?"

"God, don't shoot her."

"All right. Well, you'd better get your hands inside Rico then, before the bastard dies." He doesn't look at me while he talks. He stares intently at Maria Rosa, unwavering, hands steady. I think about changing my mind, about telling him to shoot her, but would he be able to do it before she killed me? Probably not.

So there's nothing left for it. My hands are covered in blood and dirt from when I toppled forward a minute ago. I scrub them against my jeans, doing what I can to get them clean, and then I lean over the ghostly white body in front of me and I do something neither my father nor Sloane have probably ever done: I stick my bare, filthy dirty fingers inside an open stomach wound. It feels innately wrong, and, worryingly, it feels cool. Should he really be this cold? The human body should sit at an average 98.6 degrees Fahrenheit, but the inside of Rico's stomach feels a lot cooler. This could be normal, though. I'm not a doctor. I know shit about trauma and what happens when someone goes into shock.

"Can you feel it?" Maria Rosa asks.

"No." All I can feel is intestines and a whole lot of blood that I'm assuming is not meant to be there. I twist my fingers around inside the wound, attempting to locate anything metallic, hard or sharp, but my fingers feel like they're tearing through wet paper. It definitely doesn't feel right. I think I'm killing him even quicker. My suspicions are confirmed when Rico starts convulsing even harder.

"What are you doing? What did you do?" Maria Rosa screams.

I pull my hand out of Rico, choking on panic, readying myself for the sound of the gunshot that will end my life. Do bullets travel faster than the speed of sound? I think they do. At least I won't have to hear the herald of my own demise. I guess that's something.

My heart nearly explodes out of my chest when I do hear the gunshot, though. I feel instantly numb. My breath fires in and out of my lungs in impossibly short blasts, and I flinch, waiting for the pain to kick in.

It doesn't happen.

Through the high-pitched buzzing in my ears, I can hear someone roaring in anger, and someone else screaming at the top of their lungs. That's what I should sound like. I should sound like I'm in agony, like the person screaming, and yet I feel nothing.

Hands are on me next, pulling at me, patting me down.

Rebel. Rebel's scooping me up in his arms, lifting me to my feet. Hold me to him, swearing over and over again in my ear.

"Fuck, Soph. Fuck. Fucking hell. Are you okay?"

I look down, and Maria Rosa is on her side, clawing at Rico's very dead body. She's bleeding from her shoulder, blood everywhere, all over my white tennis shoes. Her black mascara has bled all down her face too, now. She's the one who's screaming, the one who got shot. Not me. I'm okay. I'm okay. I'm okay.

"Soph! Tell me you're not hurt!" Rebel shakes me, trying to get a response.

"Yes! Yeah, I'm fine. I'm not hurt."

Rebel lets me go then. I think I might fall, but I somehow manage to keep myself upright. I watch him as he stalks around the compound, glaring into the faces of the Widow Makers who are still standing around us with their guns in their hands.

"*I* had to do that?" he hollers. "You're all standing here with your dicks in your hands? I had to get here and do that, and none of you acted?" He stops in front of Cade, his face less than an inch away from his vice president's, his chest rising and falling so fast. He looks crazy. He looks like he's about to straight up murder Cade. "What the fuck were you thinking?" he grinds out.

"I was thinking that the crazy bitch had a gun pressed against the base of Sophia's skull and I wouldn't be able to take her out without something really terrible happening. What would you have done if I'd taken the shot and Soph had been killed, you fucking asshole?" Cade shoves him. I've never seen anyone do something so risky. If anyone's going to get away with it, it's Cade, but Rebel doesn't look very happy right now. He looks like he's about to go supernova. I hold my breath, waiting for him to do something crazy, for him to smash his fist into his best friends face or pull his gun on him, but he doesn't. He glares at Cade for another few seconds, and then turns away from him, facing me again.

Maria Rosa writhes on the ground, swearing angrily in Spanish. She's bleeding pretty heavily, her blood mixing into the dirt with Rico's. Rebel ignores her, stepping over her body like she's a mild inconvenience, unworthy of his attention. He stands in front of me, his shoulders hitching up and down, a frantic energy still pouring off him in waves. "Come with me," he says.

He holds out his hand and I'm too stunned by the events of the past few minutes to object or refuse him. I take it, my legs feeling unstable as he guides me across the compound toward the clubhouse. As we pass Cade, Rebel growls under his breath. "Get a prospect to clear that shit up, man. And get her and Dela Vega out of sight, will you? Make sure they're...*comfortable*."

A shiver runs up my spine at the tone in his voice. When he says comfortable, I know he means something else entirely. He opens the door to the clubhouse, muttering under his breath when he surveys the place and finds it void of all life. We weave between tables and abandoned chairs, making our way toward the bar at the back of the room. Once there, Rebel opens another door into a back room. The small, dusty space is filled with torn-open boxes containing bottled beer, empty milk crates and cleaning equipment. The shelves on the right hand wall are a jumbled mess of spirits and...and *guns*. Guns, just sitting there like casual objects that don't hurt, maim, kill. Rebel lets go of my hand and picks up a small, silver handgun, sliding it into the waistband of his jeans at the base of his spine. "Come here," he tells me, gesturing me close. I move to his side, not sure what he could possibly want to show me in here aside from the weaponry and liquor. "Look," he says. "Pay attention. There's a small catch up here, right in the corner." His hand moves to the very top corner of the wall by the shelves. Sure enough, I see what he's referring to—a small, black switch in the shadows. I would never have noticed it if he hadn't pointed it out.

"See if you can reach it," he tells me.

He's much taller than me, but I'm still tall. I have to stand on my tiptoes but I can just about graze the smooth metal with my fingertips.

"Press it," he says.

When I was kid, my favorite thing to do on a rainy Sunday afternoon once we got home from church was to watch Indiana Jones with my father. I have awful images of some terrible booby trap springing into action if I do what I'm told and hit this switch, but I know that's ridiculous. Rebel wouldn't be telling me to do it if it would be bad for me. My nerve endings still crackle when I press my fingers against the catch, though. A loud clicking noise cuts through the tense silence, making me jump. I jump even more when the wall—what I thought was the wall—swings back to reveal yet another door. This one is made of steel, looks reinforced, and has no visible handle or keyhole. To the left, a narrow keypad sits on the wall, glowing softly in the darkness.

"Watch," Rebel tells me. "The code is One Seven Six Three." He punches the code into the keypad as I observe, my arms wrapped around my body. I'm starting to feel really shaky. Maria Rosa's arrival and Raphael's presence is catching up with me. I feel like the world is crashing down on my head and I have no means of stopping it, of holding back the tide.

The keypad is silent as Rebel presses the keys. He hits the green enter button and the door chunks and releases. Rebel doesn't allow it to open properly, though. He closes it and holds his hand palm-up to the keypad, giving me a tight-lipped smile that holds absolutely no humor. "Now you," he says. "Show me you remember the code. I need to know you can open this door."

He's incredibly intense. He's clearly so stressed he's not really functioning, and yet at the same time there's an eerie calm resting over him. It's way more frightening than if he were simply raging mad. I slowly punch in the access code to the door and hit the green button afterward, just as he did, and the door swings open.

"Okay. Good. Follow me." Rebel moves through the door into the pitch-black darkness beyond. I hesitate a second, but then follow behind him, unwilling to push him even a little while he's in this state. The heavy steel door closes behind us, and suddenly I feel like I'm trapped in a tomb. A dark, impenetrable tomb that I have no way out of. My chest tightens ever so slightly, the first strains of panic setting in, my heartbeat noticeably quickening.

"Rebel?"

His arms are immediately around me, his chest up against mine, his lips pressing against my forehead. He holds me in the dark and breathes. I can feel the impossible speed of his own heart beating against mine, and I know he's having trouble holding himself together.

So strange. He always seems so unflappable, like a bomb could go off right next to his head and he'd still be able to think straight.

"Fuck, Soph," he whispers. "Just…I can't…"

My cheeks burn, my head swimming as he draws me even tighter and crushes me against his body. Is…is he this freaked out because of *me*? Surely not. Despite Maria Rosa, Raphael, Hector, dead Bron and dead Rico, I'm selfish enough to enjoy this fleeting moment in the dark. My fear has completely vanished. With his arms around me, it feels as though nothing bad could ever reach me here. Such a bizarre feeling.

"If something like this happens again, Sophia, this is where you come. You hear me? You come straight here. Promise me."

"But where—"

"Promise me!"

"Okay, yes. I swear it. I promise."

Rebel draws back, pulling in a deep breath. He lets me go then, and the fear returns with the force of a freight train. It's amazing to me that I can be this terrified as soon as his presence is gone, and yet no more than a second ago I felt so safe.

Rebel moves around in the dark, not fumbling, apparently sure of his surroundings, and then the blackness vanishes as a strip light flickers on over head, casting a stark white light over everything inside…inside the huge office we're now standing in. It's immediately obvious whose office this is. On all four walls, white board material has been scribbled over from the floor to the ceiling; nearly ninety percent of the scribble is mathematical in nature, and absolutely none of it makes sense. Well, not to me, anyway.

Two large desks, one at either end of the room, are piled with papers, and some seriously expensive looking computers sit among the madness, apparently gathering dust. In between them on the far wall, a huge server stands like a tall, dormant monolith, all dark metal and LEDs that remain unlit.

Rebel watches me as I walk around, taking in the weirdness of the place. He leans against the tidier of the desks—I assume it's his— observing me like I'm some sort of endangered zoo exhibit. "What is this place?" I ask him.

"This place is bomb proof. This place can withstand all hell breaking out around it, and no one will be able to get in. This is where you're safest if something bad goes down."

"And the computers? The server?"

"Information. It's all just information. Bank accounts. Blackmailing. Satellite images. P.I. reports. *Burial locations.*"

"So this...this is what you have on people. All of the dirt you've gathered over the years. This is all leverage?"

"Yes."

In the distant recesses of my mind, I recall Julio discussing some files Rebel was holding over him, which was why the guy drove across the state in the night to pick me up from Hector's place: Rebel was bribing him.

I quit my investigating, leaning against the other desk, facing him. "Very valuable, I'm sure."

"Yes."

"And you showed me how to get in here. You'd trust me in here all by myself?"

He nods. "You think you're a flight risk, Sophia, but you're not. You're as invested in me as I am in you."

"I don't think so." I don't know how invested in me he thinks he is, but regardless...I don't want it to be true. Caring about this man will only get me killed; that much is obvious.

Rebel looks away, focusing on the wild, red text marking the wall by his head. He folds his arms across his chest. "You know why you resist me so much, Soph?" he whispers.

I narrow my eyes at him, trying not to let him see what I'm thinking. "Because you're rude and arrogant, and you left me alone in a cabin for ten days?"

He smiles softly, allowing his gaze to fall to his feet. "Nope."

"Oh no? Well, please enlighten me, then. Why do I resist you so much?"

"Because you're in love with me, and you're afraid."

"*What?*" I consider picking up the large rock that's being used as a paperweight on the desk next to me and chucking it right at his head. He is such an asshole. "You are dreaming, my friend," I inform him.

"We're not friends. We're much, much more than that and you know it."

"Jesus, you...you just have no shame, do you? Where do you get off saying stuff like this?"

"I find shame is usually a wasteful emotion. It occurs after an event or certain actions have taken place. There's no sense in beating yourself up over something you can't change or effect, right? I think you're actually uncomfortable because I say what I think. I don't sugar coat anything. And I've never been afraid to admit what I want, Sophia." He rubs his fingers over the stubble on his jaw, piercing me with those blue eyes of his. "You, on the other hand... you're afraid of admitting anything to anyone, ever. Must be exhausting."

I don't answer him. I don't really know what to say. I want to be stubborn and hard with him, tell him he couldn't be more wrong and he should keep his half-baked theories to himself, but I am so done. I don't have the energy to fight or bicker with him. And besides, it's becoming harder and harder to deny that what he's saying isn't actually the truth. Fuck him. Fuck him and his ability to see right through me. Rebel starts to laugh. "You don't need to say a word, sugar. You know it's true, and so do I. I can wait, though. If you ever feel like being honest with me, I'm ready to hear it."

His voice softens out at the end of this statement, the laughter slipping away. He sounds muted, soft, almost pensive. I want him to put his arms around me so he can hold me and make the whole world go away again, but won't that just be proving him right? Instead, I turn away from him.

My eyes land on a file sitting on the overflowing desk. Scrawled across the front of it in black, blocky capitals is one word: MAYFAIR.

"What's Mayfair? Is that, like, a code for something? A place?"

Rebel sighs heavily. I can hear his boots grinding against the bare concrete underfoot as he paces the length of the room; he takes the file from me and places it back on the pile of disorganized binders and papers. "It's a name. A guy back in Seattle. Cade's been looking into him."

"Is he connected with Hector and Raphael?"

"No. He's not someone we need to worry about right now, Soph. We have other things to take care of. Namely Maria fucking Rosa."

CADE

I learned how to waterboard somebody without killing them back in Afghanistan. There's a trick to it. If you pour the water too fast, shove the rag down their throat too far, you'll drown them straight away. If you go too easy on them, they can hold their breath and they'll never break. As I fill up a four-gallon canister with water from the outside tap close to the clubhouse, I spend a moment reflecting on how little Maria Rosa is going to like this. That's probably the understatement of the century. She's going to fucking *hate* it.

The roles are usually reversed in situations such as these. She tortured the ever-loving shit out of me when she found me and Rebel snooping around her place in Columbia. I spent three days strapped to a chair while she tried to ascertain if I was there to try and kill her or not. The experience was a frustrating one for her. Being in the Marines, you learn how to withstand torture. You learn how to keep your damn mouth shut and give nothing more than your name and rank, and Maria Rosa wanted me to be screaming. I was a disappointment to her in the beginning, but then later she confessed my silent stoicism turned her on. Wasn't long before she was straddling me, grinding herself up against my cock, torturing me in a different way. That seems like a long time ago now.

She was unconscious when I carried her into the barn and down into the hidden basement, making sure to bolt the hatchway behind me when I came back up for the water. I trussed her up pretty tight when I tied her to the single, lone wooden chair down there, but she's a wily one. No, not just wily; she's a goddamn contortionist. I've had first hand experience of that. I'm yet to fuck another woman who can fold herself up into a pretzel the same way Mother can.

I try not to think about all the things Maria Rosa can do that other women can't as I carry the canister of water back to the barn and unbolt the hatch. Down the stairs I carry the carton, along the badly lit corridor, water sloshing out onto the dusty concrete, onto my boots, not thinking about the things Maria Rosa can do with her tongue.

Jesus.

When I enter the very last room on the right, the woman in question is slumped forward in the chair, chin resting on her chest, a thick river of blood drying down her arm and her leg. She looks like she's out cold, but if there's one lesson I've learned in this life, it's do not trust Maria Rosa. She's a master manipulator. I'm sure Rebel would have a couple more very choice names for her, too.

She fucked with the club.

She fucked with my sister.

And now she's fucked with Sophia.

It takes a lot to get Jamie to the point where he'll bury you as soon as look at you, but we're past that point now. I kind of feel sorry for the woman. He's not going to go easy on her. Not even a little bit.

I pull the rag I found behind the bar in the clubhouse from the back pocket of my jeans and lean against the wall with the huge container of water at my feet, tearing the rag into long strips. This is where the boss finds me.

He's not looking too shit hot.

"You tried to wake her up yet?" he asks.

I shake my head.

"All right. Let's get this over with. I shouldn't have reamed you out. I know you were only looking out for Sophia. I lost it. I'm sorry."

I shrug.

"Don't give me that shit, man. You'd have lost it, too. You'd have blown a fucking gasket if that had been Laura."

I lock up at the sound of my sister's name. We'll go weeks, sometimes months, without speaking of her. Both of us just knows that she's the reason we're here though, neck deep in stinking shit that makes us both sick, drives us both crazy. We'll never be able to get out until we find out what happened to her, one way or another. And then make whomever is responsible for her disappearance pay. Dearly. That day will be the day Jamie and I lose our souls for good.

I shoot him a shitty look. "So you're comparing Sophia to her now, is it? You really must love her or something."

Rebel's eyes narrow so dramatically, they almost disappear entirely. "Maybe. Maybe not."

I throw one of the balled up pieces of rag at him, and it hits him in the face. "You're so full of shit, man. I saw the way you looked at her the second she climbed on the back of your ride in that fucking disgusting yellow dress and I knew we were all doomed."

The ghost of a smile flickers across his face. Bending to pick up the piece of rag I threw, he grunts. "Like I said. Maybe. Maybe not."

Maria Rosa groans. It's not the kind of groan she'd fake. She'd want to sound sexy, even through her pain. No, this is the kind of groan someone makes when they're in agony and their head's not working right. Rebel turns his attention to her, and I catch a glimpse of how much trouble she's in...

If the look on my brother's face were to be categorized by a single act of violence in recent history, it would be codenamed Hiroshima. He's going to kill her. I can read that fact in every line of his body. He's wound so tight, I'd be surprised if he even waits for her to wake up before he starts on her.

"Are you okay, man? I can do this on my own if you need me to?"

"And you won't end up fucking her brains out instead of teaching her a lesson?" He lifts both eyebrows at me, clearly convinced that this is what will happen if I'm left alone in a room with her.

"I can get it done." And I can. Ever since Laura went missing, the closest we ever came to finding her was at Maria Rosa's place. Too many people told the same story. Too many people said she had her. Rebel and I turned her place upside down once Mother let us have free rein, but there were those three days. Those three days where she was deciding if she hated or loved us. She could easily have had any girls she was hiding in her villa relocated, never to be seen again. Buried, thrown into a ditch somewhere for wild animals to pick their bones clean.

Yeah, I can get this done.

I know he won't agree to leaving me here with her, though. Even if he did think I was capable of making her talk all by myself, his conscience wouldn't let him. He'd never ask me to do something he wasn't prepared to do himself. That's how we've ended up in this situation so many times. *Together.*

Maria Rosa stirs again. She makes a delirious, gurgling kind of sound at the back of her throat, and then her head lolls back, eyes finally shuttering open. Rebel clenches his jaw, readying himself. This is not going to be fun for anyone involved, but he's angry enough right now that it won't trouble him as much as usual.

"Good sleep, Mother?" he growls. Slowly, he begins to pace around her in a circle, wrapping the torn piece of rag around his fingers over and over again. "You're planning on gracing us with your presence, I see."

Maria Rosa's pupils dilate, desperately trying to focus on her surroundings. She's very clearly having problems, though. She's lost a lot of blood. And she was hysterical before that anyway. God knows where they were before they came burning out of the desert, but something serious obviously went down. Serious enough to end Rico, anyway. Rebel told me about the last time he saw Maria Rosa in Vegas— that she and Rico put on quite a show for Carnie. She fucked Rico right in front of them. Even back in Colombia, it was fairly plain that Rico was in love with her. It was only a matter of time. The woman can never resist a man who fawns over her, no matter if she's attracted to him or not. She'll fuck a guy just to make him purr. From the show she put on as Rico was dying, however, I wouldn't be surprised if she actually had some form of feelings for the guy. Not real feelings, of course. She's not capable. But some sort of...*tolerance* for him. More than she ever felt for me, that's for sure. She repeatedly said she was in love with me, but you don't attempt to stab someone you're in love with to death. At least not in my limited experience.

She blinks drunkenly up at Rebel, and everything seems to hit her all at once—Rico dying, threatening Sophia...she probably remembers Trader Joe's and the heat we pulled from the DEA last, because an ashen, gray color sweeps across her face, turning her into a ghost.

"Oh, my, my," she whispers. Her words are slurred but still audible. "I suppose this is quite ironic, no?"

"Not really," Rebel replies. "I'd say it was more...*karmic retribution.* Do you believe in karma, Mother?"

"Only the bad kind." She leans forward and spits on the floor—blood and saliva mixed together. "I'm guessing you're very angry with me, my love."

Rebel laughs. He tips his head back and howls so loud I'm sure people in town can hear him. "You could say that. Yes, I'm just a *little* bit mad with you. Can you blame me, though? I mean, you sent men in to a grocery store wearing Widow Makers' cuts and you had them kill a whole bunch of innocent people. That wasn't very nice, was it?"

Maria Rosa rolls her eyes. "It was a warning. Nothing more. The cops were never going to charge you. That's why I had that fat one wear the president's cut. The police would do a little digging and pull up the club's details, see your handsome face and know it was the wrong guy, and they would figure it out. That's why I chose Los Angeles not New Mexico, you spoiled little shit."

"*I'm* the spoiled little shit?" Rebel grinds his teeth. I just stand there, leaning against the wall, waiting. At some point one of them is going to drag me into this, but until then I'm quite content sitting it out on the sidelines. Rebel shakes his head, scowling at Maria Rosa.

"You're petulant, and you have the stones to call *me* spoiled? I came to you for help in good faith, and now look at where we are."

"We are here because you have no fucking sense of humor, Rebel. We're here because I messed up your pretty girlfriend's hair. Kind of pathetic, don't you think? She's still pretty. She still has all of her hair. Even though she killed Rico."

It was plain to see that Rico was on borrowed time when they pulled up in those cars, but trust Maria Rosa to see it that way—Sophia didn't save him, therefore she killed him. "There will be...consequences for that," she wheezes.

"Oh? Consequences? You really think you're getting out of here alive?"

"I do. I don't think you're a cold-blooded killer, Rebel. More's the pity. I would respect you more if you were, I think."

There's only so much of this baiting Rebel will take before he eventually does snap. I've only seen it once before, and it was messy and brutal, and it took three weeks to get him to calm down afterward. If we can avoid that outcome, that would be great, but Mother loves to wind a guy up. She teased and tormented me for hours and hours at a time. Difference is, I handled it. Rebel will wrench her head off before he puts up with this much longer.

He slides his hands into the pockets of his jeans, looking around the room like he's never been in here before and all of this is new to him. Like we haven't had these kinds of conversations plenty of times before, with plenty of different people. This is the first time we've had a 'chat' with a woman, but then again Maria Rosa hardly counts. She loves to skin people, for fuck's sake. She's wielded the blade herself more times than any of us can count.

Rebel walks over to the container filled with water and plunges the rag he's holding into it, so that his hand comes up running water everywhere. There's no showmanship, no bravado. No drawn out production over it. He knows it's pointless trying to scare Maria Rosa, just like I do. This won't be about terrifying her into telling us everything she knows about Hector. This will be us bending her to our will, and then when bending doesn't work, breaking her. And *then* she'll tell us.

That undoubtedly makes us evil people, but this is a very unique situation. Maria Rosa really fucked up with that stunt she pulled. She should have gone back to Colombia and continued trafficking her blow. Threatening Rebel and then framing the club? Yeah, that was never going to end well.

"Open wide," he tells her.

"I'm not normally so eager to please, but...whatever you say, my love." Maria Rosa opens up, unflinching, unwilling to show that she's even slightly afraid. Sophia reminds me of her a little, in a way. While Soph is admittedly a little more intimidated by our fucked up world, she wears this look of defiance wherever she goes, like she's ready to throw down should the need arise. I respect that about her.

Rebel jams the rag into Maria Rosa's mouth. He then gestures for another one from me. I wet it in the container and hand it over. That goes into her mouth, too. And then another. And another. He's hitting her with this hardcore. She really won't be able to breathe in between rounds of water being poured into her mouth, but it doesn't look like Rebel cares. He kicks out Maria Rosa's feet from underneath the chair and grabs her by the ankles, pulling her down so that her head is tipped back. The position looks sexual, especially with Rebel standing with one leg either side of hers, but it's not. He stands like that in order to lift up the heavy water container without tearing open his stitches anymore. Maria gives Rebel a dead-eyed smile around all of the material he's forcing into her mouth.

He smiles back, holding her face in both of his hands. "What happened to you, Mother?" he asks. He genuinely looks like he wants to know, though there's a touch of madness to him. "Something fucking *terrible* must have happened to you." She looks up at him, not even attempting to speak, not even attempting to answer his question.

He tilts the water canister, and we begin our adventure.

No matter who you are, no matter how strong your will, if someone pours a gallon of water into your mouth when it's stuffed full of rags, you're going to choke. You're going to splutter. You're going to half drown. Maria Rosa does all of these things as Rebel pours and breaks, pours and breaks with a grim efficiency.

Predictably, she doesn't tell him a fucking thing. Eventually she loses consciousness. Rebel straightens, glaring down at her limp, soaked body, and shrugs his shoulders. "Well. I guess that was a pointless exercise."

He sounds way too calm. Frankly, it's a miracle that he's functioning on any rational level at all. "You're not gonna wake her up?"

Rebel grunts, tips his head back, closes his eyes, and then draws in a deep breath. "No. No point. If I carry on with this shit, I won't be able to stop until she's fucking dead."

At least he knows this. That in itself means he's keeping his shit together. Kind of. "Can you stay with her?" he asks. "When you leave, have Carnie come sit down here and watch both rooms. Make sure Mother and Dela Vega are behaving themselves. In the meantime, do what you have to. Find out what she's doing in New Mexico, and why the hell she thought it was a good idea to come here."

"Has to have something to do with Ramirez, right?"

Rebel slowly shakes his head. "Maybe not. Remember that DEA agent she wanted me to sort out for her?"

"Yeah."

"Well, it took me a while to put the pieces together, but the DEA agent that picked me up yesterday...?"

"Lowell? She's the same agent? *No way.*"

"Way."

"What are the chances?"

"Pretty high, actually." Rebel rolls his neck, opening his eyes. He looks at me, the cold blue of his irises almost the color of ice. "She's in town because of Ramirez. He and Maria Rosa are the two biggest drug importers into the United States. It's normal that the same unit would be investigating them both. She must be the big, swinging dick, this Lowell. She's a viper for sure. Find out what you can about her from Maria Rosa when she wakes up. In the meantime, perhaps you could dig the bullet out of her, please? I don't feel like finding her dead tomorrow." He cocks his head to one side, surprise chasing across his face. "Weird. I actually mean that."

SOPHIA

I don't go to Bron's funeral.

I didn't know her, and besides…if I were to look at her oddly shaped figure, wrapped up in layer upon layer of white sheets, I'd know it looked odd because the poor woman is without her head, hands and one of her feet. I'm doing my best not to recall the image of her hanging by her one remaining foot as it is. And the club still doesn't know or trust me. A funeral is a deeply personal event. I don't want to intrude.

I spend my time reading in the cabin instead. Pretending to read. Really, I'm trying not to be hyper aware of the fact that Raphael is so close. It does not feel safe with him no more than a hundred feet away. Rebel assured me he was tied to a freaking chair, that there's no way for him to get to me, but the hairs on the back of my neck keep standing on end every time I hear the cabin settle.

Later, when Rebel returns from mourning with his club, he tells me to grab a coat and follow him. For the first time since he came and collected me from Julio's compound, he tells me to climb on the back of his Ducati and hold onto him tight.

When I was a kid, maybe about seven or eight, Dad took me to see Santa Claus at Christmas. He took me to an expensive department store, the kind that hire genuine white-haired old men with real beards—men who didn't feature on any sex registers. My father sat me on Genuine Santa's knee, and he told me to tell the old man everything.

Santa had gentle brown eyes, the eyes of a Labrador or a Golden Retriever. When he asked me what I wanted more than anything in the world, I told him I wanted to be just like my big sister. My parents loved her more. She got all the best presents. She was really smart, so she understood what our father was talking about half the time. I wanted to be just like Sloane.

I felt that way for a long time. I was about sixteen before I realized that the eternal quest to Be Like Sloane was a futile one, and it was just as well being Alexis as it was being anyone else. Better, in fact, because being myself required very little effort, and being Sloane took so much concentration that I couldn't concentrate on anything else.

I think about what Sloane would or wouldn't do a lot, though. I'm think about what she would do now, as Rebel places his hands over my mine, wrapping his fingers around the trigger of the gun I'm holding. The gun he told me to take hold of back in the storage room in the bar.

In the distance, somewhere out toward the highway and civilization beyond, all that remains of the daylight is a hazy pink band, burned orange where it meets the horizon. The sky overhead is darkening with every passing minute, revealing a deep, rich blue, scattered with the pinprick of stars.

"Hold it like this. Make sure you keep your finger straight along the length of the gun up here. Don't curve it around the trigger just yet," Rebel tells me.

"This what they teach you in Motorcycle Gang 101?" I'm full of snark, since he dragged me out of his cabin in the dusky night air and refused to tell me where we were going or why. I shouldn't have been surprised that he would lead me out into the middle of nowhere and want to teach me how to shoot a gun.

Little does he know I can already fire a gun perfectly well. Dad taught me when I was a teenager, the same way he taught Sloane. I keep this information to myself. Having Rebel's chest pressed up against my back, feeling his warm breathing in my ear, is too nice to pass up. It feels wonderful, actually. I lean back into him, feeling him tense and then ease at the contact.

"No," he tells me. "Not motorcycle gang 101. Military School. Very different organization, I assure you, sweetheart."

It slips my mind from time to time that Rebel even went to Military School. And then I remember the dozens and dozens of pictures on his father's wall, and it seems entirely normal that the man standing at my back fought for his country and defended his people. Being a protector is second nature to him.

"Now, when you fire," he tells me. "Don't pull at the trigger. Don't jerk it. Squeeze it softly. Don't hold your breath. Just inhale..." He removes his left hand from over mine and places it over my sternum, above my belly, making a satisfied sound at the back of his throat when he feels my ribcage rise. "Good. Now, nice and steady. When you breathe out—"

The report of the gun fire shatters the silence in the desert. Fifty feet away, the rusted Budweiser can Rebel balanced on top of a round fence post jumps into the air—a direct hit. No more than two seconds later, the echo from the shot comes back to us, weakened by the distance it's traveled but still bracingly loud. Rebel grunts. He sounds more than a little bemused. Using the index finger on the hand resting over my chest, he digs me in the ribs, burying his face into my neck.

"Cheat," he growls.

"I didn't cheat. I did what you told me to."

"But you've already done it before, haven't you? And you had me thinking you were completely ignorant to the workings of a gun."

"I did no such thing. You just never asked."

"Hmmm." He stabs me with his index finger one more time, making me squirm. "Come on, then. Show me. Show me what you're made of."

He must trust me implicitly. Without a backward glance, he sets off toward the fence line, collecting beer cans from the ground as he goes. The loaded gun in my hand could easily be used to put an end to him, but he knows me. He knows how I feel about him, irrespective of whether I'm ready to admit to it or not.

I watch as he stoops and collects two more cans. I'm not prepared for the wall of emotion that hits me sometimes, for absolutely no reason. He can be doing the most inane thing—scratching at the stubble on his chin. Talking to Cade. Spinning a pen absently in his hand. Picking up beer cans for me to shoot—and I'll be hit with this sensation that just feels so damn...*huge*. Like it's taking me over, ferocious and unstoppable. Like it would be impossible to run from, no matter how hard I tried or how badly my lungs burned, or how painfully my legs ached.

When he straightens, Rebel finally glances over his shoulder at me and he smirks. "You okay?"

"Yeah, I'm totally fine. Why? Why wouldn't I be okay?"

More smirking. "Because you've got that look on your face."

"What look?"

"The look you get when I've just made you come really hard and your ears are still ringing."

Blood rushes to my cheeks. Man, this guy. He has some nerve. "I don't get a look when you make me come."

"Sure you do. It's like this." He tips his head back slightly, mouth open just a fraction, his hair falling back out of his face, his chest heaving. He looks incredible. And he does look like he's just had the best sex of his life. I'm struggling to keep myself in check. A very large, turned on part of me wants to command him to remove his clothes at gunpoint. *Slowly.*

Rebel's grinning when he lowers his head to look at me. "Sweetheart, you think I'd ever quit fucking you unless I knew you were satisfied? That face is how I know I've done my job properly. It's the most beautiful, sexual thing in the world. I've memorized that lust-filled, sex-doped expression in great detail, which is why I recognized it two seconds ago when I caught you staring at my ass."

"Oh my god, I was not staring at your ass!"

He just laughs, turning his back on me again so he can carefully start balancing the beer cans on the tops of the fence posts again. "Why not? I have a great ass."

I can't deny that—he most definitely does have a great ass. It's just frustrating that he *knows* it is all. "Just get the cans up there, jerk."

"Yes, ma'am. If you hit all of these without missing, I'll treat you to something very special. Would you like that?"

"An Audi R8?"

He shoots a raised eyebrow over his shoulder at me. "You really don't know the meaning of inconspicuous, do you? A car like that would draw some serious attention around here. Either way, no. No Audi R8 for you. You'd get a far better ride out of what I'm offering, anyway." He looks positively evil as he says this. There's no doubting what he's referring to. I'd have to be stupid to miss the innuendo. He oozes sex when he's like this—intense, fixated and just a little wild. He's much calmer than he was earlier. His nervous tension pours off him just as strongly as his lust, though. He's not in a good place. Flirting with me might be a great way to distract himself, but I get the feeling he wouldn't follow through on any of his promises. He's just trying to rile me.

I decide to put the theory to the test. Purely out of curiosity, of course. Not because holding a gun in my hands always makes me feel heady with power, and his rather obvious comments have me tingling all over my body. "Okay," I say. "If I hit all...*five, six,* seven cans, you'll give me the ride of my life, huh?"

Rebel places the final, seventh can on top of one of the fence posts, straightening up. From the way he sets his shoulders, pushing them back, the cheeky glint in his eye turning very, very serious, it's clear he didn't expect me to take up his challenge. "Yes, ma'am. You can't miss a shot, though."

"What happens if I miss? No crazy sex for me?"

"Oh, no." He stalks toward me, something dark and dangerous now playing in his eyes. "There'll be sex for you alright. The tables will be turned, though. It'll be your job to please *me*. Your job to blow *my* mind. You'll have to do absolutely anything I tell you to, without question. That's a big responsibility." He pauses, crossing his arms over his chest. "I'm not so sure you can handle it."

I pull a face, shaking my head, trying to laugh off the highly sexual tone in his voice, but I can't. His words, the thought of obeying him, doing as he tells me, working to please him and sacrificing my own pride in order to do so...it's weirdly appealing. I want him to use me. In some perverse way, I want to lose this challenge so I can find out exactly what he would have me do. It would be the most eye-opening experience. I'd sure as hell know an awful lot more about his desires and kinks if I submitted to him like that. And if there's one thing I've ever been sure of in my life, it's that Louis James Aubertin the third has many, *many* desires and kinks he hasn't introduced me to yet.

"I can handle it," I say softly. "I can handle anything you throw at me. You should know that by now."

A smile twitches at the corners of his mouth. "Kidnapping, maybe. Having a gun pointed at your head, sure. But this? *Me*, uncut and uninhibited? Not holding back? I don't think so, sweetheart. *I think you'd be terrified.*"

He neglected to mention Raphael. After Raphael, nothing will ever scare me again. Certainly not Rebel. He told me himself that he would die to protect me. Common sense dictates that he would then be the last person to hurt me. Intentionally, at least. I smile, pouting a little. "I guess we'll see then, won't we?"

Rebel stands at my side like a statue carved out of marble as I line up my first shot. He doesn't look at the tin can waiting to be knocked off it's post; he stares at me instead. The heat of his gaze is palpable. Swallowing, I take aim, adopting the stance he had me shoot in before. Both my hands are on the gun, even though I can probably make it with just my right hand for support.

"Don't miss, sweetheart," Rebel says. "I promise you, I'm holding you to this deal. Whatever the outcome, you'll have to deal with the consequences. Do you agree?"

"Sure. Why not."

"All right, then. Better get to it." He holds out his hand, palm up, an invitation to get my ass in gear and get firing.

I try to be too cocky as I let off the first round. The can makes a high-pitched, metallic *ting*ing noise and leaps into the air. Dad would have given that a ten. The second shot is only an eight. The bullet hits the can slightly off center, but the impact sends it flying all the same. Rebel clears his throat. "Nerves getting to you?"

"Nope. You're just standing way too close, soldier boy. Why don't you back up a little?"

Rebel laughs. "Afraid you might hit me?"

"Perhaps. I mean, I doubt you could take any more injuries at the moment. A gunshot wound to the leg would likely finish you off." I make a show of aim the gun at his right leg, but the bastard doesn't seem concerned. He paces toward me instead of moving out of the way, until he's standing right in front of me. For some reason, following him with the gun seems like a smart thing to do. The muzzle ends up pressing into his chest, and he's not blinking, breathing, moving. He's staring at me and it feels like the whole world has stopped.

"If you're planning on shooting me, you should probably do it now, Sophia."

"Why now?" My hand shakes. It feels as though I have a jackhammer pushing blood around my body and not a fragile human heart.

"Because today...today has been one of the worst days of my life. If you wanted to put me out of my misery right now, I wouldn't stop you. On the other hand, tomorrow I might wake up full of piss and vinegar and want to go hunt down Hector Ramirez. I might decide to go round two waterboarding the woman we're hiding under the barn. And I might just feel like asking you to marry me. A good night's sleep can really change a man."

"You waterboarded Maria Rosa?"

Rebel lets out a bark of laughter. He looks away, scanning the horizon. A dimly burning sliver of copper, rapidly disappearing below the rocky ridgeline in the distance, is all that remains of the sunset. He squints at it, frowning. "I just implied that I've been considering asking you to marry me, and you object to the fact that I dumped a bucket of water over a woman who threatened to kill you not only seven hours ago."

"Yes, but you were joking about the proposal part. I know you were, asshole." He has to be joking. Has to be. There's just no way he's being serious.

He steps forward just a little so that the gun digs deeper into his chest. There's a weighty look in his eyes. I don't know what to make of it, of his body language, of anything that's happening right now, but I know I'm beginning to feel a little freaked out. He's so close, I can smell him—entirely natural, and yet addicting at the same time. I can't get enough. "Why am I not being serious?" he asks. There's no doubt that he's looking and acting very serious, but my brain just won't comprehend the prospect that he's not fucking around.

"Because! You know. You're a smart guy. There's no way you'd ask a girl to marry you if you'd met under the circumstances we did. Especially only a month after that meeting, too."

"Why not?"

Oh my god. I'm beginning to think he's lost the plot. "Because you're meant to date for a couple of years, see if you like someone before you marry them, Rebel."

He pulls a dismissive face, rolling his eyes. "It takes you *years* to know if you like someone? Sounds like horse shit to me."

"Of course not. That's not what I—" I pause, take a deep breath, then start over. "There are steps you're meant to follow. You're meant to live together first."

"You're already living with me."

"You're meant to meet each others' parents."

"You've met my dad. He's a total ass-swipe but you've *met* him. And anytime you want, I'd be happy to meet your folks. You know, I scrub up well in a good suit." He winks at me.

I ignore him, because this is all far, far too absurd. "You're out of your damn mind. You're being a jerk, pushing this because you know I'll say no and you just want a reaction out of me."

"If thinking that makes you feel better, Sophia, then that is totally okay. Though, I think in the profession you were studying back in Seattle, the way you're acting at this moment might be termed as *avoidance."*

"Get the fuck out of the way, Rebel. Am I supposed to be shooting these cans or not?" Even as I snap at him, I realize that what he's saying is true, though. I am deep in the grips of avoidance. But, hell, shouldn't I be? I mean, what a crazy, half-baked, insane thing to bring up. We barely know each other. And I'm more than a little intimidated by the man. If and when I get married, it's going to be to someone who didn't pay a considerable amount of money to buy me from a Mexican skin trader. I'm going to know my future husband intimately. I'm going to know his favorite color and what he thinks of Stevie Knicks. I'll have heard stories from his childhood so many times already that I'll know them by heart. We'll have traveled together and explored different countries, seen and done so much together that...*that it will feel like we've already had all of our adventures? That we have nothing left to learn about each other?*

It hits me like a punch to the gut. People place so much emphasis on getting to know your partner before you agree to spend the rest of your life with them. Perhaps...god, I don't even want to think it, but I can't seem to stop myself. Who ever said knowing someone inside out is a good thing? Could that be why so many marriages fail? Because there are no adventures left to be had? No secrets to be uncovered? No mysteries left to untangle?

I shake my head, forcefully shoving the thoughts out of my mind. What the fuck is wrong with me? My father would have conniptions if he knew what was going on in my mind.

Rebel's wearing a shit eating, I-*know-what-you're-thinking-and-I-like-it* look on his face when I climb back out of my head. "You wanna shoot the cans, that's okay with me. You forget...I get to strip you naked either way, though, Sophia. It's win/win for me."

A shiver crawls up my spine, my skin breaking out in instant goose bumps. This bet is a win/win for him, but does that mean it won't be a win/win for me, too? Would obeying him, doing what he tells me to do without question, be that terrible for me? I somehow don't think it would. "Maybe I'm...maybe I'm curious," I whisper.

"Then why bother with our little shooting lesson? You're clearly a crack shot. Why not just say, *'Jamie, I want you to take me back to the cabin, and I want you to show me what it means for you to be my master.'"*

My hand is trembling on the gun so badly that I'm suddenly worried I might accidentally shoot him. Despite the cool night air of the desert, my palms are slick with sweat, as is the back of my neck. "You told me I shouldn't call you Jamie," I say quietly.

Rebel leans in, filling my head with the smell of him. "Oh, sugar. If you were going to say those words to me, I'd definitely want you to call me Jamie. At least then, when you eventually *do* run away like any sane person would, I can replay the sound of your voice telling me that. And it will be for *me*. Not the guy who's wrestling to keep his people together. Not for the guy who didn't protect his uncle. Not for the guy who's been searching for his best friend's missing sister for what feels like forever. It'll be for the guy who came back from Afghanistan never thinking he'd find a woman strong enough or brave enough to take him on."

I lower the gun, letting it hang down by my side. "I've already told you. I'm not going to run."

"Then it looks like you're the crazy one, not me."

"Looks like it." I can't believe what I'm about to do, but I know it's happening. I'm ramping up to it, a part of me panicked and scared yet unable to talk me out of voicing the words he wants to hear me say. "Jamie, I want you to take me back to the cabin—"

Rebel moves like a whirlwind. He catches me up, wrapping his arms around me, pinning me to him so hard that it feels like our bodies are fused together. He's kissing me, then. Kissing me so intensely that pinpricks of light start exploding like fireworks behind my closed eyelids. His hands are in my hair, roaming all over my body, palming my breasts, moving over my thighs. The moment is so unexpected and fierce that I begin to wonder if I'm imagining it. My imagination has never been this good to me, though. He slides his tongue into my mouth, exploring me, tasting me, and I follow his lead.

The gun I'm holding drops to the ground, and then my hands are in his hair, arms winding around his neck, and he's lifting me up so I can wrap my legs around his waist. His hands cup my ass, holding me up. When he pulls back, he's breathing heavily, his chest heaving, his eyes bright and shining in the near darkness. "We can still have amazing sex without you finishing that sentence, Soph. Don't say something you don't mean. Don't say something you can't take back."

A frisson of fear sparks in the pit of my stomach, but that's all it is—a small nagging sensation. When I look into his eyes and see what's in store there for me, how giving myself over to him will be so, so much more, that fear fizzles out and vanished entirely. "I trust you," I tell him. I lean closer, crushing my breasts up against his chest in order to whisper in his ear. *"And I want it."*

His reaction has me gasping out loud; he grabs hold of my hair in his right hand and makes a fist, pulling my head back. "Then do it. Say it," he growls.

"Jamie, I—I want you to take me back to the cabin, and I want you to show me what it means for you to be my—my master."

A slow, wonderfully sinister smile spreads across Rebel's face. "Sophia?" he says.

"Mmm?"

"You may not want to talk about it this second, but you *are* going to marry me. You know that, don't you?"

I feel weak and helpless in his arms, but not in a bad way. I also feel safe. Protected. At peace. I know, no matter how many other men I could potentially meet in my lifetime, no matter how special they might be able to make me feel, I will never meet another man like this. I will never feel as special as the way he makes me feel. I bury my face in his neck, hiding from the truth in his eyes and the truth in my heart. I can't face it yet. It's too damn frightening.

Rebel laughs silently, his shoulders moving up and down. He presses his lips against my temple and then stoops to collect the gun I dropped on the ground. I'm still clinging to him, legs wrapped around his waist, arms around his neck, when he shoots out the remaining cans.

"Come on, sugar," he whispers into my hair. "Let's get you home. Time to show you what you've been missing.

REBEL

I take a corner, leaning my Monster into it, and Sophia's thighs tense ever so slightly. My dick is suddenly harder than reinforced concrete. Fuck Maria Rosa. Fuck Agent Lowell. Fuck Hector Ramirez and his evil piece of shit right hand man. All I care about right now is what's gonna happen when I get Sophia through the door and into my damn bed. I doubt very much we'll make it to the bed in all honesty. At this rate, as soon as we pull up outside the compound I'm probably going to be bending her over my motorcycle and fucking the living daylights out of her just to warm her up. She has no idea what she's getting herself into. No clue whatsoever.

Up ahead, the compound is lit up against the darkness like a beacon. We pass the huge tree where Carnie found Bron's body as we head toward home, and I can feel Soph judder against me. No matter how much time passes, that tree is always going to have evil connotations for her. For me, too. I'm not normally one for wantonly destroying living things, but I make a mental note to come out here tomorrow morning to take a chainsaw to the damn thing. I'll use a pickaxe to dig the stump out, and then I'll fill in the hole so it looks the same as the rest of this desolate landscape. Shame, really.

There are plenty of people milling about when we pull through the compound gates. I park my motorcycle up alongside the long line of machines behind the barn. Cade's out the front of the clubhouse smoking a cigarette. He sees us, gives me a curt nod of his head, but he doesn't come over. He'll have things to tell me—if anyone can make Maria Rosa part with information, it's Cade—but he must see the small shake of the head I give him. He'll wait for me to come find him later. After my business with Sophia is at an end.

The girl beside me has her shoulders drawn back, chin tilted proudly. She's set her jaw, and looks extremely defiant as I gesture for her to lead the way up to the cabin. She sets off without batting an eyelid.

"That woman hates me," she says.

"What woman?" I don't really need to ask, though. There's only one possible person she could be referring to. Shay needs to calm the fuck down, or she's gonna get called into my office and we'll be having words. Really unpleasant ones. Sophia jerks her head to the right, where Shay is leaning against one of the storage units, talking to Dex, one of the Widow Makers' longest standing members. She's glaring at Sophia, sending her the foulest look imaginable. She seems completely oblivious to the fact that I'm even here. When she does notice me I shoot daggers at her and she looks the other way, eyes to the ground. When I was a kid, Ryan taught me how to treat a woman. Southern manners are hard to shake off, regardless of where you end up living and regardless of how other people may treat the fairer sex. Shay's something else, though. She's enough to make me forget my manners entirely.

"You guys used to sleep together, right?" Sophia asks.

She's far too astute for her own good. I can see the awkward look on her face out of the corner of my eye; I know telling her the truth is only going to make her feel weird, but in the same vein I'm not going to fucking lie to her. I never will. "Yeah. Couple of times, back when she first showed up here. I put a stop to it very quickly."

"Why? I mean, she's a beautiful woman. You didn't think so?"

I laugh, placing my hand non-too-subtly on Sophia's ass as we climb the hill toward the cabin. "Sugar, a girl can be just about the most stunning thing to ever walk the surface of this planet, but if she's ugly on the inside then it's only a matter of time before she's ugly on the outside, too."

"So she's a bad person?"

I take a beat to think about this. "No, not bad. Just damaged. Seriously, *seriously* damaged. This club is a family, though. You don't kick out the problem child just because they have problems, right? You try and help them."

"And if they just don't want helping?"

"Then you lock them in their rooms until they start behaving themselves." I am really not beyond considering this with Shay if she continues to act like a spoiled little bitch. "The thing about Shay is she hates to lose," I say.

"And she thinks I've won?" Sophia sounds incredibly amused by this idea. I slap her on the ass. *Hard.* She stifles a cry, which has my cock throbbing in my pants. She can try and stifle her cries all she wants, but before the night is out I swear she won't be able to help herself anymore. Her throat will be sore from all her screaming, in the very best way.

As soon as we're through the door of the cabin, I have her in my arms, feet off the floor, and I'm charging across the other side of the room toward the bed. I must take her by surprise, because Sophia goes rigid, stiff as a board.

"Shit," she hisses.

I throw her down on the mattress so hard she bounces. There's a look of poorly disguised fear in her eyes as she blinks up at me, her breasts straining against the thin material of her t-shirt as she breathes in and out in quick time. "Are you afraid of me, Sophia?" I growl.

Her cheeks are stained with a delicate, rather attractive shade of crimson, as are her lips and the base of her throat. She swallows, and then nods. "A...little."

"You can't be. If this is going to work, you can't even be a tiny bit frightened." I crouch down at the foot of the bed, grabbing her by the ankles. Pulling her forward, I only let her go when her legs are either side of me, her feet almost touching the floor. I look her in the eye along the length of her beautiful, perfect body, and grin. "Sit up."

She slowly props herself up on her elbows, and then pushes herself upright so her breasts are at my eyelevel. They are so incredible—I want to tear her shirt right off her back and go to town on them, licking and sucking, but I don't. I need to make sure she understands what's about to happen first. And what will *never* happen. "Look at me, sugar," I whisper. "Look me in the eyes."

Until now she's been looking everywhere *but* at me. It's so important that she knows I'm telling the truth when I say what I have to say now, though. If she doesn't, she's likely to flip the fuck out and panic and I don't want that. I may be about to make some serious demands of her, but I want her to enjoy them all. I want her to come so fucking hard on my dick.

"Soph, tell me what you're afraid of," I say.

She bites down on her bottom lip so hard, the skin turns white. I reach up and press my index finger and middle finger against her mouth, making a disapproving sound. She releases her lip and takes a deep breath. "I'm...I'm afraid I'm not going to like not being in control. I'm afraid I won't like being told what to do. I'm afraid—I—" she stumbles over what she wants to say, but I already know what it is. I give her a moment to finish, but when she doesn't I complete the sentence for her.

"You're afraid you'll feel trapped and unable to escape. You'll be frightened, because you think I'm going to treat you the way Raphael wants to treat you. To hurt you. To take something from you that you don't willingly want to give."

She looks away. Again I reach up, but this time it's to gently turn her face back to me. "I'm not Raphael. I don't like to hurt women. I would never, *never* force you to do something you didn't want to. We're going to push your limits, perhaps, but having those limits is okay. If you honestly don't want to try something, then all you need to do is say so and that's it."

A slow smile gradually forms on her face. "So... we're going to have a safe word?"

I laugh. "Sugar, 'no' is the only word you ever need to say. 'No' should never *not* be enough." It makes the blood boil in my veins to think that she's told someone no before and it *hasn't* been enough. I'm sure she didn't welcome Hector inspecting her to see if she was a virgin. I'm sure she didn't consent to Raphael pawing all over her, breathing down her neck, telling her all the vile things he wanted to do to her. If he'd taken it further...if he'd actually... Fuck, I can't even think about that. My rage would be a brutal, swift, consuming thing.

"Thank you," she says softly. "No's good enough for me."

"Good. Now. Do you want to know what *I'm* afraid of?"

It's very rare that Sophia looks shocked. She does now, though. It's almost comical to be honest, but I can't laugh because I actually am freaking out a little. Today isn't the best day to tell her this; I know that. But the thing about perfect moments is you don't know they're perfect until they've already passed you by.

Fuck it. Here goes.

"I'm scared because I'm in love with you, and I don't know what to do about it." I sound confident as all hell when I tell her this, but my head actually feels like it's about to implode. I only manage to sound that way, because it's true. I *am* in love with her. It's fucking inconvenient, and a genuine surprise to me, but it's true.

Sophia's eyes grow really round. She sits very still, not breathing or moving. Eventually, she says, "You're not joking, are you?"

I shake my head.

"Well, fuck."

"I know. Messed up, right?"

"Ha!" She stares at me, and I think she's not really taking this in. Not believing me, anyway. I can tell by the mildly angry look on her face. "That's really low," she says. She laces her fingers together, gripping tightly, her knuckles blanching. "Why would you do that? Why would you tell me that?"

"Because...I've never told anyone before. It seemed like the right thing to do."

"You've never told anyone you loved them before?"

"No. Never."

"What about your..." I know she was going to say my father, and I know she then realized how stupid that would be; I watch it all play out on her face. "What about your Uncle, then?" she says. "What about Ryan?"

"Nope. Never. He was a pretty stiff kinda guy. I know he loved me in his way, but he never said it. I think he would have kicked my ass if I'd have told *him*."

"And there were never any girls you dated? You...you never fell in love with any of them?" She's beginning to sound incredulous. I don't know if I should be offended, or I should be finding her complete and utter disbelief entertaining.

"No. Never been in love."

"But you're..."

"I'm what?"

"You're insanely hot! I just...I can't..."

"Lay back on the bed, Soph."

"What?"

"But we're not...you just told me that you're in love with me. I can't—" Sophia covers her face in her hands, shaking her head from side to side. She's not coping well at all with this new piece of information. I stand up, crack my neck, and then I push her onto her back, eliciting a strangled scream from her.

"What the fuck? You—"

"I am your master for the night, remember. It's time for you to start doing as you're told."

She goes still again, staring at me—seems that's all she's done the past fifteen minutes, like I'm some strange, alien creature she can't possibly comprehend—and then she lets her hands fall either side of her on the bed. "Okay," she says. "Okay, fine. Show me."

I head for the bureau on the other side of the room, slide open the top left drawer, and take out a pair of scissors. They're old. Really old. They have Winchester Gun Co. engraved on the handle, and they're really fucking sharp. Sophia's face goes blank when she sees them. She doesn't object, though. She doesn't get up and make for the door. She remains where I left her on the bed, watching me cautiously.

"What are you going to do with those?" she asks, her voice flat.

"I'll show you. We're going to go through some rules, though, sugar. Are you going to obey them?"

"Shouldn't I probably know what they are first?"

"No, you shouldn't. That's the whole point." I've only played this game with three other women, and nearly every single one of them hesitated here. It's not in a person's nature to strike bargains or agree to things without prior knowledge of their responsibilities beforehand. However, Sophia shocks me when she doesn't miss a beat.

"Okay, then. I'll obey your rules." Her voice doesn't waver. She means what she says, that much is clear, and the effect that has on my body is insane. I've never been so proud in all my life.

"Good girl. Rule number one: when I tell you to do something, you do it immediately, without question. That one's simple. Number two: don't speak until you're spoken to, or there will be consequences. Number three: you don't come without my permission. Simple, right? You think you can handle that?"

"Yes. I can."

"Okay. From here on out, we're operating under these rules. Shall we begin?"

"Yes." Her response is barely loud enough for me to hear, but I can see it in her eyes: she's intrigued. I'm sure Matt-the-boring-ex never did anything even remotely off the wall; this is probably going to be a real education for my poor little Sophia. I make my way back to the bed, scissors in hand, and I climb up onto the mattress on my knees beside her. She lies still, watching the sharp, silver object in my hand with just the right amount of trepidation to tell me she's concerned about what comes next.

I start at her right ankle, taking hold of the cuff of her jeans and then opening the scissors, sliding the lower blade beneath her clothing. Sophia sucks in a sharp breath but remains still, just like she's meant to.

There's understanding on her face now—she knows what I'm about to do, and in truth she looks a little relieved.

The scissors cut through the denim material easily; I could probably just run them upward and slice through from her ankle to her waistband in a few short seconds, but where would be the fun in that. This is a sensory experience, after all. The sound of the scissors cutting through one inch at a time is half the fun. And Sophia feeling the cold, hard metal against her warm skin is another very big part, too. She gasps the first time I lay the flat of the lower blade against her calf. I don't leave it there long. I don't want the metal to heat up, and besides, too much contact will desensitize her. She'll become used to the sensation and it won't be shocking anymore.

When I reach the middle of her thigh, I go even slower. She's breathing fast, not looking at the piece of metal in my hand or what I'm doing to her clothes. She watches me, her mouth slightly open, the tip of her tongue darting out to wet her lips, a slightly doped up look in her eyes, and it's all I can do to stop myself from forsaking the scissors and tearing her damn clothes off with my teeth.

My hard on is digging into my jeans, caught up, beginning to throb like a motherfucker, but this is too delicious to stop. I will wait until the pain reaches unbearable levels before I quit my little game and rearrange so that things are a little more comfortable. Sophia tenses a little when I make the final cut through the right hand side of her jeans, right at the top, through her waistband. Folding the material away from her leg, I see her lacy black underwear for the first time and my blood starts roaring through my body, all chasing through my veins, charging in one direction: to my cock. Before I know it, I've reached that unbearable level of pain and I have to adjust my dick. Sophia watches me do it, looking shy yet hungry at the same time. I can't wait to get through destroying her clothes so I can bury my tongue in her pussy. I can't wait to taste her come all over my tongue, sweet and delicious and all mine. And I really can't wait 'til she's digging her fingernails in my back, desperately trying not to make a sound, to not displease me while I fuck her so hard her whole body shakes.

I lean down and place a feather-light kiss on her exposed hipbone, warring with myself as I fight not to take things further. To kiss her lower. A little to the left. A little further down again. I know she's feeling the same anticipation I am when she angles her hips up a few millimetres; she catches herself and freezes almost straight away, but I sit back on my heels, giving her a warning look.

"Careful, sugar. That nearly counted."

She opens her mouth, wants to say something, but yet again she catches herself. She's good at this game so far, but things haven't even begun to get difficult for her yet. Not too long from now, it's going to take everything she's got to stay silent, and I am going to relish the moment when she breaks one of my rules. It's going to be absolutely fucking perfect.

I cut the other leg of her jeans off her body, watching her struggle to keep still the entire time, and then I take the scissors to the flowy shirt she's wearing. I cut down the arms, and then straight down the middle, biting back a smile every time she twitches when the cold metal makes contact with her belly, her arm, her chest.

"Get up," I tell her. "Stand here, in front of me."

She climbs out of the ruins of her clothes, leaving them behind on the bed, and it's almost like she's leaving behind the scared, frightened part of her. I gather up the material and dump it on the floor at the end of the bed, and then I sit on the edge of the mattress, surveying her in her underwear.

She doesn't cover herself or hide. She simply stands there, waiting for my next command. She's good at this. Perfect, in fact. "Come here," I say, opening my legs so she can stand between them. She takes two steps forward so she's right where I want her. There's only a flicker of doubt in her eyes when I raise the scissors and slowly slide the blade beneath the lacy material of her panties at her left hip. The soft snip of the metal cutting through the lace is the only sound in the room. I cut the material at the other hip, too, and her panties flutter to the floor, nothing to hold them up anymore.

Now she gets antsy. She shifts from one foot to the other, pressing her thighs together, and I tut. "You want me to punish you, don't you, sugar. You're asking for trouble." Again, she wants to speak but she doesn't. She frowns at me instead, her fingers curling into fists by her sides. She's self-conscious. God knows why, she has the most incredibly sexy body, but she is, I can tell. She wants to keep me from seeing the one part of her that no one ever sees. But I have seen her. I've gone down on her often enough to be on very good terms with that part of her body. I'm willing to put good money on the fact that her ex never went down on her. Not properly. He should have made her feel comfortable with her body. She doesn't know that her pussy is beautiful, that I could happily look at it all day long as I made her come, and she would have a fight on her hands if she tried to stop me.

I take the scissors and run the point from a couple of inches below her belly all the way up until I hit the under wiring of her bra. She knows what comes next. Her hands make fists again and this time they don't uncurl. She looks up, away from me, eyes fixed on a point on the wall straight head. Her shoulders lift up and down rapidly, like she's afraid I'm going to cut her. She knows I won't, though. She's hardly a shy woman. She'd be waling on me in a second flat if she thought I was going to do her any harm. I love that about her.

She's still focusing on the wall when I cut through the slender strap between the cups of her bra, freeing her breasts. "Take it off, sugar," I growl. Her eyes meet mine again as she obliges me, sliding the thin straps that I've left intact over her shoulders and down her arms. Completely naked, she stands in front of me like a statue, not moving, not saying anything, doing exactly as I told her to. Her obedience is remarkable, given that I know she wants to cover herself up. I place the scissors on the floor and kick them under the bed so they're out of the way, and then I tell her what I want from her next.

"On your knees, Soph. Be a good girl now."

She gives me a sharp look, eyes narrowed, but she only takes a moment's pause before she's lowering herself to her knees. I'm thinking she must be pretty pleased with the fact that her pussy isn't at my eye level now, but little does she know that's about to change.

"Good. Now, open your legs for me, sugar."

"But—" She clamps her mouth shut as quickly as she's opened it, but it's too late, the damage has already been done.

"Oh dear..." I send her my most fucked up, smug, wicked looking grin. "Looks like someone broke a rule."

"Oh come on, I didn't mean to. I—"

"You did it again. And here I was, thinking you were doing so well." I try my best not to laugh when I catch sight of the mortified expression she's wearing; she must have been counting on the fact that she wasn't going to break my rules, and now it looks like she's done it twice.

She wants to defend herself, to say it wasn't her fault, I provoked her, but she manages to stop herself from speaking this time. Crying shame, because racking up three individual punishments in under a minute would have been a record.

"You know I have to teach you a lesson now, sweetheart. I can't let that slide. I would if I could, but...y'know...rules are rules and all. Spread your legs for me, princess and I'll go easy on you."

Sophia rolls her eyes and sighs, presumably resigning herself to her fate. Without another word, she does as I've told her, opening up for me. She doesn't just open a little ways either. She pushes her legs out as far as she can do in this position, exposing herself to me.

"Good girl. Now lie back on your heels, so they're still underneath you but your back is arching away from the floor." She does as she's told again. In this position, her breasts are close at hand for me to palm as I sink down to the floor and proceed to go down on her.

Some men like to drive fast cars. Some dudes go fishing. But this, right here, giving head to Sophia, is my favorite pastime. I know she loves it, even though she likes to think it's embarrassing. It's fucking hot. She's fucking hot. I'm painfully aware of the fact that I'm fully dressed as I stroke my tongue slowly across Sophia's clit. But this is part of her punishment. I'm not going to get naked with her now. I'm not going to fuck her either, no matter how badly my balls are aching. I'm going to tease Sophia, send wave after wave of pleasure shooting through her body. I'm going to make her sweat and writhe and moan, and when she comes it will be the best orgasm of her life. And after, when she's sated and limbless, sleep rolling over her, I'm going to tell her that next time I'll stop right before she climaxes if she misbehaves herself. And I will leave her like that without a second thought.

So this is what I do. Soph's attempt to stay still and keep quiet is a valiant one, but in my head I guestimate it's a mere four minutes before she completely loses it. She doesn't even seem aware that she's bucking and grinding her hips against my mouth—which incidentally drives me fucking insane. She's so fucking beautiful. I watch the sheer bliss on her face as I continue to use my tongue to bring her closer and closer to coming, and for the first time since I was fourteen years old I nearly end up making a mess of my pants. She's practically tearing the floorboards up with her bare hands when she finally comes.

It's the most spectacular, amazing thing to watch. Her back arches off the floor, chest heaving, thighs clamped firmly around my head, and she screams. She screams loud enough that the guys down in the clubhouse must now either assume I'm murdering her or that we're having ten-out-of-ten, hard core sex.

When her body stops shaking, Sophia looks up at me out of half-closed eyes and scowls. "I'm in serious trouble now, aren't I?" she says breathlessly.

I laugh, and then I slap her thigh, which doesn't seem to amuse her as much as it entertains me. "Oh, fuck yeah, girl. You have absolutely no idea what I get to do to you now. The only thing that will save you now is that tattoo we talked about."

"No way! I am *not* getting tattooed."

"We'll see." I crawl up her body, placing kisses on her hot, sweet-smelling skin. I'm practically planking over her when I reach her mouth.

"I think you should be inside me now," she pants through our kisses.

The way she says it, the way those words sound coming from her full, biteable lips, almost makes me cave. I stay strong, though. "Sorry, sugar. You were a bad girl. Only good girls get what they want."

I leave her there on the floor, naked and still panting.

REBEL

Cade's not in the clubhouse. Normally after taking a girl up to my cabin for a couple of hours and then reappearing looking frustrated as fuck, I'd garner a few catcalls from the other Widow Makers, but tonight the mood is overly drunk and sombre. After Bron's short and simple funeral, no one's in the mood for jokes. They're in the mood to get fucked up and fight.

Three chairs and one table have been smashed by the time I manage to make it across the clubhouse bar and up the back stairs to the handful of bedrooms we have set up there. No one lives here permanently. The Widow Makers have either chosen to live in town with their families, or they have rooms in the many outhouses that make up the compound. That's probably why people think we're some sort of fucking sex cult. Cade has a place above Dead Man's Ink in town, but he won't have gone back there tonight. Not without speaking to me first. He'll be holed up in the one room that's permanently reserved for him on the top floor, waiting to spill whatever bullshit lies Maria Rosa told him when I left the two of them alone.

I lay my fist against the last door on the right, not surprised when Cade opens it right away. He must have heard my boots coming down the corridor. A gift from the U.S. Marine Corp: the ability to hear a man sneaking up on you from a mile away.

Semper Fi.

My brother in arms looks absolutely exhausted. He steps back so I can enter the room, which is sparse and OCD neat. He claps me on the back, giving me a tired smile. "You look much better than you did before, man. I think you got out of there at the right time."

"Did she say anything else?"

He shakes his head. "Nope. She did try and convince me to fuck her, though."

"What is wrong with that woman? She gets shot and waterboarded, and in the next breath she's trying to get you to stick your dick in her?" Cade gives me a rueful look that tells me it might have been worse than that. "Jesus. I don't think I want to know," I tell him.

"I'm sure you don't. Come on. Let's do this." Cade knows where we have to go next. He knows what has to be *done* next, too. Raphael Dela Vega has polluted Widow Makers ground for too long already. I won't have him here, freaking Sophia out, causing trouble amongst the club members. They know Hector Ramirez's right hand man is in one of the holding cells underneath the barn. It won't be long before someone's suggesting we chop the motherfucker's extremities off and send them back to Ramirez in ziplock baggies.

The guy has got to go. No way are we sending him back to his employer, though. No. No fucking way is that happening. If I'm honest, I'm all for the chopping off extremities and leaving them for Ramirez to find, the same way he did with poor Bronwyn, but we don't have time for that. Gunshots fired? A convoy of strange, unlicensed, shot-to-hell black cars burning out of town, headed straight for us? It's a goddamn miracle that Lowell woman isn't hammering down the gates already. There was nothing to be done about him until dark, though. With a long range scope—paranoid perhaps, but a possibility—it would have been all too easy to spot a couple of guys wrestling with a noncompliant Mexican guy in broad daylight. Now we just have to hope that if Lowell is out there and she's got people watching us, they don't have heat imaging or night vision. If they do, we're gonna be fucked.

There's a goddamn riot unfolding in the bar downstairs as Cade and me sneak out the back. Normally I'd start knocking heads together, but it's better for everyone involved if the guys continue raising hell here instead of following us. Outside, the desert air is cold and the sky is an explosion of stars.

Cade jogs across the courtyard—there's still blood everywhere. I should make Maria Rosa come clean up her fucking mess before I even consider setting her free—and opens the barn door, slipping inside. He holds the door open for me, and then we're shrouded in pitch-blackness. A pale yellow flame is struck into existence, which sends long fingers of narrow shadows stretching up to the barn rafters. Cade looks like some sort of horror movie character as he holds the tarnished zippo he's lit up to his face.

"You want me to turn on the overheads?"

"No. Would only draw attention. Dark is better."

I'm regretting my words two seconds later when Cade is falling over sideways, crashing into me, hissing under his breath. He goes down hard, almost taking me with him. The zippo skitters out of his hand, skidding across the roughcast concrete floor, though the flame remains lit, guttering and then strengthening again.

"What the hell, man?" I grab hold of Cade by the shoulder, trying to pull him up in the half dark. He grunts, and then there's the sound...the sound of a second person moaning? What? No one else should be in here. No one else should even know we have people in the basement. My hand's reaching for the gun in my waistband when Cade swears loudly.

"Fuck, no. Damn it, it's fucking Carnie."

"*Carnie?*"

There's more moaning. Cade gets to his feet, moving his considerable bulk out of the way, and then I can see Carnie too in the meagre light being thrown off by the zippo. Sure enough, he's flat out on his back, a two-inch long gash along his right temple. His eyelids flicker open, but even from here I can see his eyes themselves are not working properly, don't seem to be focusing on the men standing over him.

"What happened?" Cade demands. "What the hell are you doing up here, passed out cold, man?" He shakes Carnie hard, which seems to do the trick.

"Uh...I was...fuck. I was...heading down to take some food to Mother and the other one. I opened the padlock on the hatch and he...he sprang out. He had a broken chair leg in his hands. He must have hit me over the head with it."

When I first walked back into the clubhouse and Cade told me Ryan had been killed, it took me a beat to process what he was saying to me. Took me a minute or two to comprehend what he was telling me. Not so this time. As soon as the words are out of Carnie's mouth, I'm in fight mode, already predicting what will come next. Dreading it with every fibre of my being.

I grab hold of Carnie by the collar of his cut, pulling him off the ground so my face is in his. "How long? How long ago?" I yell.

"I don't...I don't know. What time is it?" Carnie's still struggling to string words together. Means he was probably hit over the head pretty hard. That also means he could have been out for a considerable amount of time, too. I let go of him and he drops to the ground like a sack of flour.

This cannot be happening. It just can't. *"Fuck!"*

Cade draws his gun and sets his jaw. He knows what this means, too. Raphael Dela Vega is an unhinged bastard with no sense of self-preservation. He won't have fled the compound. Not yet. He's been fixated on one thing and one thing only for a long time now, and he won't leave here until he's gotten what he's been dreaming about.

He has been dreaming about Sophia.

SOPHIA

When night falls over the desert, it suddenly feels like the world ceases to exist. Out there, beyond the lights and sounds of the compound, all drunken shouting and the furious roar of motorcycle engines, there's nothing more than a sea of black ink and an endless void that stretches for as far as my mind can imagine in every direction. No, there are no roads or general stores. No dive bars, and no all-night diners. The compound feels so very isolated and alone. It kind of freaks me out.

My body is still humming from Rebel's ministrations when I get up and draw the blinds on all the windows. God knows where he's gone. I didn't really get a chance to ask him before he fled the cabin, looking very pleased with himself. He knew exactly how cruel he was being when he decided not to stay and have sex with me. Can't have been pleasant for him, either, but still... the guy is evil.

I'm grinning like a moron as I think this, though. Grinning so hard my face hurts. He's turned me into some sort of pathetic teenager, which is ironic because I was never like this back then. In high school, I was driven by the need to excel in my schoolwork, and definitely not to pursue the attention of boys. And now here I am, turning my back on my studies in order to be with the most unsuitable person on the face of the planet.

But, in saying that, maybe he's not the most unsuitable person. If just that one thing about him were different, he would be prime take-home-to-meet-the-parents material. He's intelligent. He's a gentleman (for the most part). He was in the army. He went to MIT, for fuck's sake. But then the kicker...he's also the head of a motorcycle gang. What would Mom and Dad say if they knew what I was doing right now? A pang of guilt sideswipes me out of nowhere as I really take on board what they probably believe has happened to me by now.

They have to believe I've been murdered.

There isn't a way in this world they would ever believe I just decided not to come home when given the opportunity. So I mustn't have had that opportunity. They must think I was stabbed or shot, or worse, that I was raped and beaten to death.

God, I am the worst person on the face of the planet to leave them wondering like this. My heart feels like a lead balloon sitting heavy in my chest as I find new, un-shredded clothes to put on.

I should call them. I should just stop being such a fucking coward, and I should tell them I'm okay, even if I end up hurting them by not going back to Seattle. Straight away. Not going back to Seattle *straight away*. I will have to go back at some point. Don't I? I can't hide here forever.

The t-shirt I've stolen from Rebel's closet is clean and soft and smells deliciously of him as I pull it over my head. My moral compass starts spinning, then. Why can't I stay here for a while? At least until everything with Ramirez dies down. I have excellent grades. I could always go back to college next year if I want to. There may even be a college in New Mexico that—

I can't help but smile as I hear the cabin door creak open. He thought he was such a smart ass when he high-tailed it out of here, leaving me on the floor, needing so much more of him. And now look. He's back within ten minutes, no doubt ready to teach me a lesson. I get half way through pulling the t-shirt over my head, but then there are hands on my hands, stilling me. I'm half naked, only my head and shoulders covered by the soft, dark material. Something about that is so kinky. I'm essentially blindfolded for all intents and purposes. He could do anything to me and I would never see it coming.

"So," I say breathlessly. "You changed your mind. Will this be part of my punishment?"

"Mmm-hmm."

His stubble grazes me across my shoulder blades, my skin immediately turning to goose bumps as he places his lips against the curve of my neck. Slowly, his hands travel from mine down my arms until they're hovering just above my breasts. I want him to touch me. I want him to touch me so badly. I arch my back pressing my breasts upward, catching my breath in my throat, waiting for him to gently slide his palms downward, following the swell of my body.

However, when he does move his hands down, it's not gently. He takes hold of my breasts, grabbing with rigid, calloused fingers, and then he squeezes so hard I'm momentarily blinded by the pain.

"Ahhhh! What...*what the fuck?* No! Stop!" For a second, through my confusion, I think that this is the real punishment Rebel was talking about and I am frightened. Very, very frightened. And then it hits me. There's no way Rebel would ever handle my body like that. Like he hates it and he wants to hurt it. I may not have been with him for years and years, I may not know what his favorite color is, or what all of his childhood stories are, but I know he would never do that to me. Never in a million years.

Which means...

Terror is a living, breathing thing, snaking its way through my insides.

Oh, god, no...

Oh, god, no.

My whole body locks up tight when I hear the sound of very familiar, very evil laughter in my ear. "Oh, I knew you would have such a pretty little cunt. I knew you would love me pinching your perfect titties like this."

Raphael.

Raphael is here, with his hands on me, touching me. Hurting me. I try to drag in a breath but it's impossible. My ribcage feels like it's in a vise and I'm never going to wriggle free. My brain eventually connects my difficulty to breathe with the fact that Raphael has wound one of his arms around my chest and is squeezing tightly.

The next three seconds are a blur. I tear the t-shirt away from my head, which leaves me completely naked. Better naked than blind, though. I thrust my elbows backward, slamming them into Raphael's body, contacting with his side and his arm. He doesn't let go, though. If anything, his grip grows even tighter.

"GET THE FUCK OFF ME! LET ME GO!"

"I won't be letting you go, princess. Not this time. This time you're mine. Struggle, bitch. Fight me. Come on...make me believe it." I can't see his face but I can hear the sneer in his voice. He's loving the fight almost as much as he hates me. Because he does. He *despises* me. He's the sort of man who hates all women, purely because of their sex. I know nothing I say is going to get me out of this situation. I'm going to have to fight my way out of it, and I'm going to have to be smart about it, too.

I'm gripped by panic and fear, but somehow my brain is still working. Through everything that's happening, feeling trapped and ultimately terrified, I manage to form one coherent thought: *stop giving him what he wants.*

I fall limp in his arms.

"*Que—?*"

He's shocked at my response. Me deciding to play possum was the last thing he must have expected. I'm sure he knows that's exactly what I'm doing too, but now he has to do something with me. He has to put me down or spin me around or...or *something*. I know it, and he knows it, too.

"You think you're so smart, huh, *Puta.* So fucking smart. You always think you're one step ahead of me. Well, you're not." I realize he's right when he quickly shifts his hold and wraps one of his arms around my neck, applying pressure. Fuck. He's going to try and choke me out.

"Don't worry, princess. You'll be asleep soon. I'll have so much fun with you while you're sleeping. And when you wake up, you'll be all tied up and begging me to knock you out again. Won't you? Won't you, you little fucking slut." He braces his muscles, tightening everything as he pulls back, applying even more pressure against my windpipe. My head is already spinning. Pinpricks of light dance in my vision, floating around like drunken flies. My arms feel weak; they feel them as I scramble at his arms, trying to prise them free.

That's not going to work. Too weak. Too dizzy. No strength. Can't...

I reach further back, fingernails clawing at the ripped material of his shirt, searching for...searching for god knows what. My heels hammer against the floorboards as Raphael lifts me higher, putting even more pressure on my neck. I have seconds. Mere seconds to get out of this, or it will all be over. I will pass out, and I will never want to wake up again, knowing what he will have done to me while I am out cold. My fingers suddenly hit something fleshy, something soft. His face.

I keep scrambling, scratching, trying to claw at him, but it's not working. It's not working. Raphael starts to laugh again—a maniacal cackle that sounds unhinged. I'm on the verge of losing consciousness, but the madness in that laughter gives me the strength for one last push. One last grapple at his skin.

I feel something wet and moist underneath my fingertip, and I know this is it, my final chance. Raphael tries to swing his head around, to move away from my hand, but I butt my own head backward, cracking my skull against what feels like his nose, and then my index finger is digging into that soft area of flesh I touched a second ago.

Not bone. Not cheek. Not chin. No. My finger is digging right into his eyeball, and Raphael is screaming.

I know I've done some serious damage when he drops me like a hot coal and clutches both hands to his face. The world is suddenly in Technicolor; my head feels like it's splitting apart from the brightness and loudness of it. Blood thumps through my veins, charging full tilt as I try and crawl away from him.

"PERRA DE MIERDA!" Raphael stumbles into the wall next to him and then punches it, leaving a smear of blood on the plasterwork. I can't tell if it's from the action of actually hitting the wall or if it's from his eye. A river of blood runs down his face, and his left eyelid is swollen shut, puffy and oozing fluid. With only one eye open, he sees me on the floor and lets out a howl that chills me to my very core.

I should have moved quicker. I should have been on my feet and running as soon as he let me go. I couldn't breathe, though. I could barely see straight myself.

He falls on me, grabbing hold of my ankle and dragging me across the room toward the bed. "You should not have done that, you fucking psycho," he growls. "Are you a good catholic girl, princess? Are you?" He slaps me hard across the face, landing the blow across my ear. A high pitch whine buzzes through my head. When the sound dies down, Raphael is screaming obscenities at me, shoving his face in mine, spitting everywhere.

"I'm going to make you wish you'd never been born. I'm going fuck you raw. I'm going to make you hurt. You've brought this on yourself." He hits me again, snapping my head around with the force of his blow. With his right hand he presses my head down into the floorboards so hard I can feel the skin above my eyebrow splitting open. It feels like my skull is about to crack open. With his other hand, Raphael begins to fumble with the belt around his waist. It doesn't take much to imagine what's coming next. I screw my eyes shut, trying to think, trying to figure this out. Trying to find a way out of this. It's when I open my eyes, the sound of Raphael's fly unzipping snapping me back to reality, that I see my salvation, though.

I don't have long.

I reach under the bed.

I stretch.

I stretch so hard it feels like my shoulder is about to dislocate.

I close my fingers around cold metal.

And then I'm twisting as best I can with my head being pressed into the floor, and I'm stabbing and I'm stabbing and I'm stabbing.

I only stop when Raphael Dela Vega slumps over me, a heavy, dead weight, pumping long, hot jets of arterial blood all over my naked body.

"*Ohmygodohmygodohmygod.*" I shove him off of me, and then I'm clambering to my feet, backing away, backing up until my shoulders hit the wall and I can go no further. Shit. *Shit!* I clamp both of my hands over my mouth, trying not to see the mess I've made of Raphael. I want to look away, but I can't. My eyes are locked on the shiny pair of scissors—Winchester Gun Company—that are sticking out the side of his fucking...out the side of his fucking neck.

I pitch forward and brace my hands against my knees, and I throw up.

I don't stop until I feel hands around me. I think for a second that it's him. I think it's Raphael, that I didn't do the job properly. I start flailing, arms and legs everywhere, fighting for my life. And then I smell that smell. The one from the soft t-shirt. I smell that smell, and then I know everything will be okay.

Rebel crushes me to him, and the world turns black.

REBEL

Sophia sleeps in one of the bedrooms in the clubhouse most of the next day. When she's awake she showers over and over again, crying continually. I stay with her. I don't really know what to do to make her feel better. This is all my fucking fault. I allowed that motherfucker to remain alive and breathing on Widow Makers' ground. I should have put a bullet right between his eyes the moment I saw him standing there, but I didn't. I allowed him to live, and so in turn I allowed him to attack Sophia. She's hurting and she's in pain, and it's all because of me.

The third time she wakes and lumbers heavily to the shower, I sit on the edge of the double bed, sheets twisted up and practically knotted from where she's been tossing and turning, and I hold my head in my hands. There's nothing I can do to fix this. She wanted her freedom. She didn't want to be watched over twenty-four seven, but I shouldn't have listened. There shouldn't have been a moment of the day that I wasn't by her side, especially with that piece of shit festering away in the basement.

I allow myself a moment of weakness, and I think about Laura. It was the same with her. I turned my back for five minutes, and then she was gone. What the fuck is wrong with me that I keep letting this happen to the people around me. They always seem to get hurt. A part of me wants to shut the club down. These people that have followed me out here into the middle of nowhere, who for some reason trust me to know what I'm doing, have misplaced their faith in me. I keep proving that, time and time again.

And Sophia. She has to go back to Seattle. Like, *yesterday*.

Just the thought of what I have to do makes me want to head directly downstairs, grab a bottle of Jack from the shelf above the bar, get on my bike and then find somewhere quiet where I can drink myself into a stupor. There was a time when I probably would have done that, but I can't now. I have a responsibility to the woman quietly tearing herself apart in the shower.

I walk numbly down the hall, take my flick knife out of my back pocket, and then I twist the lock on the bathroom door open from the outside. The room is so full of steam, I can't see my hand in front of my face.

"Soph? It's me. It's Jamie." I speak loudly, so she knows I'm there. The last thing I want to do is surprise her. "Jesus, have you even got the cold tap turned on, girl? It's like a sauna in here." I know why she's scalding three layers off skin from her body, though. She feels dirty. She can still feel his hands all over her body.

This, sadly, is not the first time I've had to take care of a woman who's been mistreated by a man. It is the first time that I've felt like I'm dying myself, though.

From behind the steamed up glass shower screen, I can make out the small shape of Sophia, curled up in the corner of the tiled shower. "Can you...can you just..."

She wants to ask me to go away. She's trying to ask that of me, but she can't seem to finish the sentence. I should be a gentleman and give her what she wants. Walk right back out the door, lock it again, and give her the space she craves. But I can't. Instead, I open the shower door and I climb right in there with her, fully clothed. T-shirt, hoody, jeans, sneakers. I leave it all on. Me stripping off my clothes would be a shitty idea, even though I have zero intention of trying anything on with her.

I'm soaked the instant the stream of boiling water hits me. Sophia looks up at me, arms wrapped tightly around her body, knees drawn up to her chest, and I can tell there are tears running down her face in amongst the beads of water from the shower head. "What are you doing?" she mumbles.

I smile sadly down at her. My throat feels like it's swelling fucking closed. She looks so small. So vulnerable. She stabbed Raphael eleven times before she drove those scissors into his neck, but to look at her now you wouldn't think she was capable. I'm really fucking glad she was.

"Just checking in," I say softly. She doesn't reply. She leans her forehead against her braced arms, her body shuddering. Fuck. I've never felt like this before. I've never felt this...useless. Even when Laura went missing, I still felt like I had a purpose: Find her. Bring her home. Apologize. Sophia's sitting right in front of me, though. I haven't lost her in the same way I lost Laura. Bringing Sophia home is a different task altogether.

I lean against the wall and slowly slide down it, not making any sudden movements, until I'm sitting on the floor next to her. I don't touch her. She must hate me. She must blame me. She has every right to. I told her everything would be okay, and it was anything but.

We sit there in silence for a long time, the water feeling hotter and hotter with every passing moment. The skin across Sophia's shoulder blades turns from a violent scarlet to a bruised looking purple. She doesn't seem to notice when I slowly adjust the temperature of the water from blisteringly hot to something a little more manageable.

We sit some more.

Eventually, I feel the need to break the silence. "I'm going to drive you home tomorrow," I say slowly. "I'll drive you myself." She doesn't look at me, but I can feel her tensing, though; I know she must have heard me. "It's...for the best. I don't want anything else happening to you. Not because of me. I can't—I can't tell you how sorr—"

"You don't want me anymore."

I stop talking, turning my head to fully look at her properly. *"What?"*

"You're sending me away. You don't want me anymore," she says. It's really hard to hear her over the constant battery of the water against the slate tiles, but I can just about make out what she's saying.

"No...no, of course I want you, Sophia. Fuck, I..." My heart feels like it's being stomped on repeatedly every time it beats. How can she think that? How can she honestly think I don't want her anymore?

"I probably disgust you," she says.

Oh, god. Being stabbed at Ramirez's place hurt. Being tasered by Lowell was breathtakingly painful. But *this* pain? This pain makes me feel like I'm dying. I would hurt less right now if someone took a knife, slammed it into my chest, and twisted with all their might. "You're crazy if you think that, sugar. You have no idea. I...*I am so fucking proud of you.*"

Slowly, she raises her head, peering at me sideways, a blank look on her face. Her hair is plastered down her cheeks, her neck, her back in dark, wet streamers. "How? How can you be proud of me? He nearly..."

"Because you defended yourself. You didn't give in. And he didn't get what he wanted from you, Soph. You didn't let him. It takes so much strength to do what you did." I mean every word. Since I started buying these women from the skin traders, I've come across so many girls who were overcome by the dark places they found themselves in. A lot of the time, giving up felt safer than standing their ground. That was how they coped, how they stayed alive. I'm pretty sure giving up wasn't something that even crossed Sophia's mind.

"I'm not strong," she whimpers. "I'm not."

I want to smash my fists into the wall, but that won't help her. More violence is the last thing Sophia needs in her life, and so I wrap my arm around her shoulders instead, pulling her to me. "You are the strongest fucking person I know, okay. Don't you ever fucking doubt that. And you do not disgust me. I fucking love you, okay? I fucking love you."

It's as though she finally gives in and breaks all at once. She's stiff as a board one second, resisting me, and the next she's crumpling, falling slack, and then climbing into my lap, throwing her arms around my neck, clinging onto me as though her very life depends on it.

Since I raced up to the cabin yesterday, my heart trying to climb up and out of my mouth, I haven't been able to touch her properly. She's flinched every time I've gone near her. Seems that her reluctance to have any sort of physical contact with me has passed now, though, and I am so fucking relieved I could cry.

"It's okay, Soph. It's okay." I gently stroke my hand over her hair, my eyes clenched tightly shut, and she cries into my soaking wet clothing, fisting my t-shirt in both her hands. When she stops crying and just breathes against me, I turn off the water and wrap a towel around her body, and then I carry her back to the bedroom.

Sleep takes hold of her.

When she wakes up, it's dark and I tell her I have a job for her. Confusion clouds her face as she looks at the pair of heavy-duty gloves I'm holding out to her.

"Why are you giving me those?" she asks.

"Because digging's hard work. I doubt your hands are already covered in calluses, sugar." She doesn't ask me why she's going to be digging. She gives me what can only be described as a baleful look, but then takes the gloves and gets dressed in the jeans and sweater I brought down from the cabin for her.

Outside in the courtyard, a huge bonfire is blazing, cracking, spitting, sending burning hot red and orange embers spinning upward into the black night. Cade took a chainsaw to the hanging tree. I couldn't do it, so he stepped up and got it done. A small crowd of Widow Makers, Brassic included, stand around the fire with beers in their hands. They watch with silent respect as Sophia and I walk by. When she first came here, the guys were dubious of her. New people, especially pretty young women, are always cause for suspicion around these parts. But now she's not the girl who lead Ramirez back to New Mexico, to our doorstep; she's the girl who killed Raphael Dela Vega. That will forever earn her kudos with my guys. Even Shay nods her head as we pass. There's no anger in her eyes tonight. She just looks weary, and I kind of get it. Being as angry and as confrontational as Shay is twenty-four hours a day, seven days a week, must be exhausting.

Soph and I climb up into the Humvee, and she doesn't mention it but she must know I have Dela Vega's body in the back, out of sight. I drive thirty minutes south, heading in the opposite direction from the spot where we buried Bron yesterday. Lowell hasn't paid us a visit yet but there's every chance she's having the compound watched, so I don't turn on the car's headlights. I just drive in a straight line, my eyes accustomed to the dark, and Sophia stares out of the window, her thoughts clearly weighing heavily on her mind.

When we stop and get out of the car, the night air smells weirdly like eucalyptus and something else. Something sweet that I can't put my finger on. The dark shadow of Sophia's form moves quietly around the car, where she opens the rear passenger door and takes out the two heavy shovels I put there before we set off.

"How many times have you done this?" she asks me. Her eyes shine brightly, full of pain and sadness, but they're dry. I get the feeling I won't see her crying over Raphael Dela Vega again; the firm set of her jaw and her ramrod straight posture speak volumes.

I want to lie to her and tell her I'm new to this. That I haven't been burying people out here in the desert for *years* now. But I can't. What would be the point in deceiving her? She's a smart girl—maybe too smart for her own good—and she must already know the truth. I want her to know me, dark, evil things included, and telling her otherwise would only be misleading her. "Too many times to count, beautiful girl."

"Were they…were they all men like Raphael?"

Nodding, I drive the point of my shovel into the ground. "And worse. Far, *far* worse."

She seems to think about this for a long moment, the sweet smelling breeze lifting tendrils of her dark hair about her face, and then she nods. "Okay."

"Okay?"

"Yes. If they were worse than Raphael, then they deserve to be here. I get it."

I'm not prepared for her acceptance of this knowledge, so I don't have anything to say at first.

The two of us start digging; it's not long before Sophia sheds her sweater, stripping down to the thin t-shirt I gave her to wear, and I'm naked from the waist up. We're both sweating and breathing heavily by the time the hole is deep enough to dispose of Raphael's body.

I purposefully haven't covered him up. He's all blood and horror and loose-limbed madness as I heave him out of the back of the Humvee and drag him under his arms to the grave we've prepared for him. His skin a strange mottled purple color, apart from where he's covered in his own dried blood, which has turned the color of rust and dirt.

"Are...are his eyes meant to look like that?" Sophia asks softly. She's glancing at Raphael's already decaying body out of the corner of her eye, as though, if she only manages to glimpse him in small snapshots, she'll be spared the true horror of what she's done. That won't do her any good, though. That's why I left him uncovered. She *needs* to see him. She *needs* to come to terms with the fact that she killed him.

"Yeah." I drop Raphael on the ground, and then go to stand beside her. Taking her hand, I draw her to my side, trying to stem the body-wide shivering that seems to be taking her over. "That always happens."

Her fingers feel icy and cold in mine. "Do you know why?" she asks.

"It's the potassium breaking down in his red blood cells. Makes the eyes go cloudy."

"He looks...looks like he has cataracts. He doesn't look *real* anymore." Taking a deep breath, she finally looks at him properly. "I get why you're making me do this," she whispers.

"Tell me."

"Because you want me to have closure. You want me to be the one who buries him. You want me to be the one who shovels dirt onto his body and sends him away forever. You want me to understand he's never coming back, and he's never going to hurt me again. That's why."

I don't say anything. I don't need to. She's hit the nail on the head; without this sort of closure, she'll only ever remember him with his hands on her, trying to force himself on her. He would always seem stronger than her in her mind. More dangerous. He would forever haunt her. Now, like this, broken, just a slowly degrading husk, he has no power. Yes, he looks terrifying, covered in all that blood, staring up at the star speckled night sky with his mouth yawning open in surprise, but he also looks small. Weak. Incapable of causing her any more pain.

I nuzzle my face into her hair, breathing her in, trying to transfer some of my strength to her. She's already so damn strong, but that's irrelevant. If I could carry this burden for her, I would. If I could have been the one to kill him, I would have. I *should* have. I don't ever want her to hurt or suffer any more than she has to. "Do you want me to help you?" I whisper.

She squeezes her hand in mine, taking a deep breath. "No. No, it's all right. I can do this."

She gets to work. Even after she's pulled on the gloves I gave to her at the clubhouse, I can tell she doesn't want to touch Raphael. She has to in order to get his body into the hole, though, so she steels herself and then grabs him under the arms, the same way I did when I dragged him from the car.

Raphael was a big guy, and Soph is nowhere near as strong as me, so it's not as easy for her to maneuver him to the side of the grave. She doesn't give up, though. She positions his body directly beside the gaping hole in the ground and then she straightens, staring down at the man who's plagued her dreams since that night back in Seattle.

"You were a vile piece of shit in life, Raphael. And you're a vile piece of shit now. Fuck you." She trembles as she spits on his body. Trembles as she uses her foot to shove him roughly into his final resting place. He lands face down, which feels highly appropriate. A strange sense of pride washes over me as my girl tosses the first shovel-load of dirt into the hole.

"My father would have a fit if he knew I was doing this," she says.

"Burying the man who assaulted you?"

"Burying him like this, face down, with no blessing and no prayer for his soul."

"Your father's religious?"

She remains quiet for a second. I know it's hard for her—she still hasn't given me her real name, and I haven't pushed for it. I know her last name is Romera, or at least her father's last name is, but even that wasn't information she volunteered. I heard him say it when she called him on that payphone back in Alabama. She still feels conflicted about parting with information that might endanger her family, and I get that... But *she* has to get that I am not a danger to her family. She *must* know that. The main threat to her family is now being covered with the dirt she's letting fall from her shovel.

I don't think she's going to answer me, but then she speaks after all, talking in muted, quiet tones. "Yeah. He's a preacher for all intents and purposes. My family are pretty devout Christians."

I had no idea about this, but it fits. When I first met her, she had that uptight air about her that spoke of a sheltered, strict upbringing. That's gone now, lost to the four winds. Now, she seems like an entirely different person.

I sit on the ground by the graveside and watch as she labors to fill it in. The work is backbreaking but she doesn't complain and she doesn't ask me to do it for her. With every load of dirt she piles on top of Raphael Dela Vega's body, she seems to become more and more confident, her back straightening, her eyes flashing with determination. When it's done, Sophia drops the shovel to the ground, rips off the gloves I gave her, and sinks to the ground beside me. My arm finds its way around her shoulders instinctively, and she folds into me, resting her head on my shoulder.

"About what you said before," she says.

"Which part?"

"The part about you driving me back to Seattle."

I cringe at the words. "Yes." It's going to hurt like a motherfucker taking her back home, but it's the right thing to do. What I should have done weeks ago instead of dragging her further and further into this mess.

"I don't want you to drive me back," Sophia whispers.

Hearing her say that is like a punch to the gut. I understand. I don't like it, but I will respect her wishes. "Okay. Public transport's out of the question, though. I need to know you've walked back through your front door okay. I'm sure Cade won't mind taking you if you pref—"

"No, that's not what I mean." She looks up at me, frowning slightly. "I mean, I don't want to go. I mean I want to stay here. I want...*I want to be with you.*"

I've known pretty much from the beginning that she was attracted to me. It was fairly obvious from the way she acted around me and how often I caught her staring. I was hardly shy about the fact that I was into her, too, though. This, however, is a huge surprise. She looks a little stunned herself.

"I thought you'd jump at the chance to get out of here, Soph. Don't you want to go home? See your parents? Your sister?" I stroke my hand over her wild, wavy hair, dreading whatever she's going to say next. I want her to be safe. I want her to be a million miles away from Ramirez and his men, even if Raphael is no longer a concern. But I also want her in my line of sight at all times, close enough that I can touch...

"I'm going to call my dad," she says. "I want them to know that I'm okay. And I want them to know that...that I'm not coming home."

"Perhaps you should think about this before you make any rash decisions."

"I have. It's all I've been thinking about for days. I don't think I can go back to who I was before, Jamie. I'm not...I not the person I used to be."

When she calls me Jamie, I feel like I *could* be the person I used to be, if I tried really hard. That would mean giving up this whole enterprise, though. It would mean admitting that Cade's sister is gone and that we're never going to find her. After so long, I think I've already come to terms with that fact anyway. Admitting it is hard, though. Admitting it to Cade would be fucking impossible. We barely talk about her anymore. He must have come to the same conclusion that I have, but she's his blood. He won't stop looking until he's found out what happened to her one way or another. And I won't abandon him.

"This club is intense, Soph. Being here means you're going to be more and more involved in the way we live our lives. Is that something you can put up with?"

"Yes. I want to. I—" She turns to face me, eyes about as wide as I've ever seen them. She's so fucking beautiful. I want to wrap her in cotton wool and keep her safe. Forever. "I want to be a part of it," she whispers.

"Be a part of the club?" This...this is guaranteed the very last thing I ever expected her to say. I still don't think I've understood her correctly. "You want to be a *part* of the club?"

"Yes. I want to do what Carnie did. I want to prospect."

"*No. Fucking. Way.*" She's gone mad. I shouldn't have made her bury Raphael. It must have caused severe trauma to her brain.

"Why not?"

"Come on. Let's get in the car." I help her to her feet, and then I'm half guiding, half dragging her back to the Humvee. She doesn't make a sound when I open up the passenger door for her and usher her inside. Slamming the door closed, I hope the loud noise will be an end to the crazy conversation, but Sophia's ready and waiting for me.

"Shay's a woman. Fee, too."

"That's correct. They are."

"So why can't I be a Widow Maker? If they can be, then surely I can be, too."

I start the engine but I don't put the Humvee into gear. I swivel in my seat so I'm facing her, desperately trying not to launch myself across the other side of the car so I can shake some sense into her. "You can't join because it's dangerous, sugar. Things with Ramirez are about to get grade A fucked up. I'm trying to make your life safer, not even more dangerous."

"Do you honestly think Ramirez is going to forget all about me now that Raphael's gone? Am I still not the only person who can testify about your uncle's murder?"

"*Raphael* killed Ryan. Raphael's now dead. There's no way to prove in a court of law that Hector ordered him to do it. That ship has well and truly sailed. The cops are never going to fix this. *I'm* going to have to fix it. *The club* is going to have to fix it. It's going to be all out warfare, and that bitch Lowell is going to be along for the ride. God knows how it's all going to end. I don't want it to end with you swinging from the end of a rope, missing your fucking hands and feet, though."

"Why are you reacting like this? I thought you'd be happy that I wanted to stay, Rebel."

Rebel. Huh. No more Jamie. That's probably for the best. I punch the steering wheel, grinding my teeth together, expecting to feel them crack under the pressure. I can't seem to think straight all of a sudden. My entire body feels hot, my senses working overtime to keep up with my rising anger. "Have you forgotten what I said to you the other day? I told you I was fucking in love with you. That means I will let you go. That means I will kiss you goodbye and I will help you pack you shit into the back of this car, and I will let another fucking guy drive you out of here. It means I will never see you again if that's what I have to do, because I love you so goddamn much that I'd rather my whole world come crashing down around my fucking ears than have you killed because of me. Go back to Seattle, Sophia. Become a psychologist. Marry boring Matt and have a ton of children. Go to book club and drink too much Sauvignon Blanc on the weekends. Get a divorce at forty and find yourself all over again. Live the clichéd, middle class life that I can't give you."

I'm blowing hard, my lungs burning when I shut my mouth. I've never really known what it is to feel like this—utterly destroyed. It's come as a complete and very unwelcome shock to me that I am going to be fucked when she goes, but she *needs* to see it's for the best. She *has* to.

It takes me a long while to realize that she's not saying anything. When I look at her, Sophia's staring dead ahead, arms folded across her chest, eyelids unblinking. She's practically vibrating with rage. Her tone is even and flat when she begins to speak; I can tell it's taking everything she's got to remain calm enough to get her words out. "Over the past few weeks, you've been stabbed, nearly bled to death right in front of me, attacked by Ramirez, shot with a Taser and arrested by the DEA. You think I wouldn't worry about you if I went back to Seattle? You don't think I would be sick to my stomach every second of the day, wondering if you're alive or you're dead? Fuck, Rebel...*you don't think*

I'm in love with you, too?"

She gets out of the Humvee, slamming the door so hard behind her that I'm surprised the damn window doesn't shatter. I watch her storming off into the desert, the pale blue of her t-shirt fading fast into the darkness as she hurries away from the car. For a moment I can't move. I can't think straight. *She loves me, too?* She loves me too. I feel like she's just punched me square in the jaw. I mean...*how?*

I finally get my shit together in time to realize that she's been totally swallowed by the near pitch-blackness outside and I should definitely find her before she vanishes for good. I get out of the car and run after her.

She's not too hard to find. Standing with her back to me, she's only made it thirty feet from the car, and she's crying. "I should fucking hate you," she tells me. "I shouldn't give a shit about you, whether you live or die, but I do. That day you took me up on the roof of your dad's place, you said something to me and it's been stuck in my head ever since. You said, 'Don't bother trying to get inside my head. It's a dark and scary place. Even I don't want to be here most of the time.' But I couldn't help it. I wanted to get inside your head, and you..." She turns around, stabbing her index finger into my chest. "You invited me in. You didn't for one second try and stop me from developing feelings for you. So why should you get to care more about me than I care about you? And why the hell am *I* not allowed to take risks to make sure *you're* okay? I have nothing to go back to, Rebel. I have a family and a college degree and I have an apartment sitting empty in Seattle, but if you're not there with me then I have *nothing.*"

I can't fucking breathe. I can't...

I grab hold of her and pull her to me, wrapping my arms around her and holding her so tight to me that she probably can't breathe either. She presses her face into my chest, clinging onto me, and we just stand there, not letting go. Not saying anything. Not moving.

This woman has turned me fucking inside out. I reach down and lift her up, my hands underneath her thighs, and she wraps her legs around my waist without question. I just hold her there.

"You want this? You really want this, knowing what it involves?"

She pulls back, her eyes slightly red and puffy. There's real grit there, too, though. So much fire. She swallows, and then says eight words that will change things for us both forever. "I want *you*. And I'm not going anywhere."

This is pure fucking madness, but I can't help grinning. One of us will end up dead soon enough, but in the meantime I'm sure things are about to get really fucking interesting. "You realize you're going to need to learn how to ride a motorcycle now, right?" The thought of her in charge of a bike is instantly hot. Her intensity breaks as a small smile spreads over her face.

"Seriously? That would be kind of badass."

"Oh my god," I groan. "You're gonna be the death of me, woman."

"Huh. And here was me thinking I would try and keep you out of trouble instead," she says softly, biting her lip.

It occurs to me how fucked up this is—the fact that we've just disposed of a body in the desert in the middle of the night, and I'm swiftly developing a hard on. I laugh like a maniac because I can't help myself. "All right, then. Sophia Romera, consider yourself the newest prospect of the Widow Makers Motorcycle Club."

CALLIE'S NEWSLETTER LOTTERY

As a token of her **appreciation** for reading and supporting her work, at the end of every month, Callie and her team will be hosting a **HUGE giveaway** with a mass of goodies up for grabs, including vouchers, e-readers, signed books, signed swag, author event tickets and **exclusive** paperback copies of stories no one else in the world will have access to!

All you need to do to automatically enter each month is be signed up to her newsletter, which you can do right here: **http://eepurl.com/IzhzL**

*The monthly giveaway is international. Prizes will be subject to change each month. First draw will be taking place on Nov 30 2015, and continue at the end of each month thereafter!!!

ABOUT THE AUTHOR

Callie Hart is a bagel eating, coffee drinking, romance addict. She can recite lines from the Notebook by heart. She lives on a ridiculously high floor in a way-too expensive building with her fiancé and their pet goldfish, Neptune. Rogue is the first instalment in her Dead Man's Ink trilogy. Book three will be coming out soon!

Her **Blood & Roses** series has over two thousand five star reviews, and features a dark hero and a kickass heroine. Book one, **Deviant**, is **FREE** right now!

If you want to know the second one of Callie's books goes live, all you need to do is sign up at **http://eepurl.com/IzhzL**.

In the meantime, Callie wants to hear from you!

Visit Callie's website:
http://calliehart.com

Find Callie on her Facebook Page:
http://www.facebook.com/calliehartauthor

or her Facebook Profile:
http://www.facebook.com/callie.hart.777

Blog:
http://calliehart.blogspot.com.au

Twitter:
http://www.twitter.com/_callie_hart

Goodreads:
http://www.goodreads.com/author/show/7771953.Callie_Hart

Sign up for her newsletter:
http://eepurl.com/IzhzL

TELL ME YOUR FAVORITE BITS!

Don't forget! If you purchased **ROGUE** and loved it, then please do stop over to your online retailer of choice and let me know which were your favorite parts! Reading reviews is the highlight of any author's day.

I must ask, though...if you do review Rogue, please do your best to keep it spoiler free or clearly indicate your spoilers clearly. There's nothing worse than purchasing a book only to accidentally ruin the twists and turns by reading something by accident!